SAVING

THOMAS GATRELL

1

2

Preface

A young couple's dream journey begins as they set out to conquer the blue depths on their quest to reach Sydney Australia from New Zealand's North Island. A journey that would prove far more dangerous and eventful than they could ever have imagined

This book is dedicated to all the Bowman Yachts workers and colleagues at Emsworth West Sussex from the early 1970's until the early 1990's

SAVING GRACE

THOMAS GATRELL

Beware of the sea

She owes you no favours

Beware of her smile

Her welcoming trait

For the costs of her invite

Can question your fate

CHAPTER ONE

My name is Phillipe Lecarre.

I think our story began yes, it was late September 1995 and I had travelled from New South Wales Australia to North Island New Zealand on a cheap one way air ticket. I was in between contracts and had some spare time and a lazy attitude of late, quite normal for a single 25 year old guy I would often tell myself.

It was good to get away for a break and re-discover some freedom for a change. The flight to Auckland went quite well though it felt good to touch down and feel the terra firma under my feet again. I don't travel too good in the air but like most people I suffer the tensions For the need of a break.

I had no return travel plans in my head and within five days of enjoying the scenery of Hawara, I met Melanie a lovely sun tanned Samoan girl living and working there.

We spent a lot of time together and gradually realized that after seven days, we were falling hopelessly in love with each other.

She worked at the sea life centre near town but we met at one of the many cafes in Hawara's market area.

She took my breath away and it wasn't long before I was suggesting that she return to Australia with me in good time.

She made no secret of the fact that she led a fairly lonely life in Auckland . As our romance grew stronger, we were soon talking about getting engaged and heading back to Aussie with her as my fiancee. The very thought was so incredibly exciting for both of us. We were inseparable and had visions of the perfect future together.

We'd gone back to that very café where we had met, just to discuss the simple romantic possibilities of what the future could bring.

Melanie like myself didn't like flying. Four years ago at the age of eighteen she had ventured by passenger /cargo ship from Tonga to take on her new agency placed position at the sea life centre, but she was ready for a change and was full of ideas. I had often mentioned my love of sailing to her albeit on a fairly part time and casual basis. When she first suggested sailing back to Sydney as a celebration cruise I thought her idea a bit naive and ridiculous to mention, but the more we discussed the possibility the more exciting the prospect grew.

Her idea of putting our cash together to buy a second hand boat seemed a very bold idea but, as we both agreed it sounded better than putting good money into more air or ship tickets. We drank a toast to our crazy adventure to be and took a walk to the nearest jewelry store which was located not far from the market square.

Melanie looked so beautiful with yellow roses in her hair and a daisy garland about her neck. It was a wonderful day and I had never felt so happy and proud to be with the love of my life.

Her diamond ring glittered in the sunlight as it shone through the trees at the edge of the market. That evening before we retired to her flat we agreed that on the following day we would start looking for our 'ideal' passage back to Sydney. I hired a small car to help with the effort and would enable us to get back to her place in the evenings.

We would try the nearest boatyards and see what we could get for our limited budget. New Plymouth is host to many boatyards and yachting facilities and we concluded that this would be the best places to start.

It was Thursday, 28th September, and Melanie had a four day break from work so as to accompany me in the search for a reasonable craft.

After three boatyard stops and much walking about we were exhausted from our efforts and decided that one day would certainly not fix this search.

Before we left at the end of the first day, we checked out the yachting brokers' windows and realized that our budget would not lean to such extravagant notions.

It was on the second day that our luck changed.

It was Friday 29th, and at around 2.00pm with a coffee in our hands overlooking the local inner bay, Melanie leaned further across the deck and, glancing carefully out across the anchorage spotted something—'Phil look, isn't that boat for sale?'.

Before I could reply, an older gentleman more like an 'old sea dog,' interrupted.

'You two looking for a boat young man?..word soon gets around!'-

He quickly pointed out that the craft attracting my fiancee's attention was in fact his own.

I glanced at Melanie, beckoning her back to the tables and ordered more coffee, three cups this time.

Sam introduced himself and as he talked and explained why he was selling his trusty craft, my eyes were transfixed at the boat even from 120 yards distant.

There was a 'for sale' sign scrawled in white paint onto a piece of plywood attached to the port side lifelines. But the rest of the details had long since worn away from seasonal periods of weather and neglect.

'She looks a fine boat and I certainly prefer wood to fibre glass that's a fact', I blurted out in fascination. 'Unfortunately sir, I fear we could never meet your sale price I think, it looks in fine shape and will more than likely be too much for us'.

Sam rubbed his chin, sipped the coffee, the froth sticking to his small graying beard and said, 'Selling my boat won't change my life but it sure will make it easier.-I can't keep up the maintenance any more, my joint's are aching and it's all too much for me now,-better somebody like yourselves get's some enjoyment out of it,--course, I can't give it away!'.

Melanie looked at me and then to Sam. She said, 'Ok, bottom line is how much are you asking?- as we have to think about preparing the boat and stocking her for a five to six day trip to Sydney'.

Sam twitched an eyebrow 'Well, she's certainly sound enough on the hull I believe, but you would need to get the rigging checked over for such a trip young man'.

I kept nodding—'So how much is she?'

He looked at us both carefully, 'I can't let her go for less than two thousand dollars I'm afraid, even though she is thirty years old'.

My expression fell down and Melanie looked back across the channel.

'I'm sorry Sam, forgive me but our budget is fifteen hundred dollars as we'll have to spend at least five hundred or more to prepare and re-insure her. I don't doubt she's a solid boat but we have our limitations. If you hang on I'm sure you will get the two thousand, it was a nice idea but we'll keep looking around'.

'Leave me your contact number young man, if she's not gone by the end of the month maybe we'll have another chat'.

Sam had disappeared after thanking us for the coffee, and Melanie sat back on the plastic chair looking quite beautiful yet ill at ease.
Resting my arms on the rail I looked back across the anchorage studying the boat in question. She was a carvel built sloop of some eight metres by my judgment, in fact quite a lot of boat for the money he was asking but, it would surely come with the age related maintenance issues that would be due.
I could make out the coamings around the cockpit, a necessary built in feature for a working yacht of her length. Without binoculars I could still tell that her original wooden mast had been replaced, a sure sign of the true age of the vessel which I reckoned to be more like forty than thirty years!—A small red flag in my head as I gazed across at her.

Somewhat disappointed and just a little bit disillusioned, we made our way down from the deck and headed back to our hire car.

Driving back, Melanie pointed out that the end of the month was in fact only two days away, Sunday in fact.

'Did Sam realize that?'--.

We both agreed that we both liked the boat even if only from a distance, and perhaps we should stop panicking, have a rest for a couple of days and see just what Sunday brings to us.

One thing was for sure, that if we were to accept to buy this boat then the price should include hauling out and inspecting the hull, keel and rudder, just for peace of mind.

Sam had mentioned that he hadn't actually sailed the boat in two years, that she had laid there on the mooring unchecked for the same amount of time. This was a grey area for me, one I would reflect upon should we get the opportunity to purchase her.

Saturday was spent lazily sitting and walking around the market taking in the warm, hospitable atmosphere. Some of the locals would wave and chat, they had come to know and accept Melanie as one of their own even though her spiritual home was of course, Tonga.

We tried not to think of Sam's boat too much, believing that she was financially out of reach to us.

The Saturday afternoon passed quite peacefully as we sat back on our beach chairs holding hands in the gap between.
No matter how much I wanted the phone to ring there was only the sound of the shoreline and of the ever circling seagulls. Maybe they knew something that we didn't.

At 4.30 pm or thereabouts we headed back to my hotel for a shower prior to slipping out to dinner. We were both ravenous. I've always likened a life close to the ocean as responsible for a good appetite.

So much fresh air to clear one's mind.

As we headed for the stairway near reception a voice called after us, 'Mr. Lecarre, one moment'. My heart skipped a beat as I could see the porter held a piece of paper in his hand-'A message for you sir, - a gentleman delivered it personally for you, I hope it's not bad news'.

Melanie looked concernedly at me and then, 'Well, tell me quickly!'

We moved over to a small aged sofa in the corner and sat down to read.

'My god, he says we can view the boat tomorrow around late morning, but no mention of the price!'—She squeezed my arm and smiled optimistically. 'Maybe he change his mind about the money Phil you think?'.

Whatever the note really meant, it never really mattered that much in some small way as I looked at her gracious and loving smile. I knew then that I had already found my true love and inspiration.

Tomorrow would be another day and just maybe, the start of another adventure. Time would tell us both.

CHAPTER TWO

Sunday 1st October 1995.

On Sunday morning we dragged our feet at breakfast just to pass some time, so keen were we to head out to view the boat at the anchorage. With two cups of coffee and a cooked breakfast under our belts Melanie signaled with her eyes at me that it was time to get moving.

With some trepidation on my part we collected our bits and pieces from my room and headed for the car park, not really knowing how this day would work out.

A fifteen minute journey soon passed with bright sunshine flooding through the clouds, a blue and white canvas creating the day ahead.

At the boatyard we were greeted by a soft, fresh breeze as we headed from the car park and found our way up onto the café deck, assuming that we would find Sam there, and we did. He was there, sitting back looking non too confident if my quick analysis served me correctly. He turned to signal a message to the woman through the open doors and at the counter beyond.

'Coffee's on the way young man'.
Melanie was already at the handrail of the deck looking in various directions with a puzzled look on her face. 'Phil where is the boat, it's gone!'.

Sam sat back on his chair and stretched his legs, giving a small yawn, 'I've been up since early, don't worry. She's in the slip having her bottom scrubbed. If you look over there to the left you can just make out the top of her mast.

I knew that you would need to see her out of the water to help you come to a decision and it's something that I have been putting off for a while, now that I'm not an active working man any more'.

We were finding it hard to contain our nervous anticipation as we quick stepped through our coffees. After all, it's not every day that one gets the chance to see a real lady's freshly scrubbed bottom!-my fiancee gave me a strange look trying to read my fresh smile!..

Within ten awkward minutes Sam eventually said , 'Come on let's not dilly dally any more, let's see if they've finished'.

I was the first out of our chairs as the moment of possibility looked before us. A two minute walk down over the rough ground between lots of small huts, Melanie hanging on to my waist belt, led us down to the slipway and a check on reality. We all stopped thirty feet short of our target to take in the view, and I took a quick picture with my digital camera, just for the record.

'That's her my friends, freshly scrubbed and soaking wet, say hello to the 'Lady Grace'. Melanie and I looked at each other as we wandered around the 'Grace'-. There she was, resting on her keel and supported by two large lifting strops from the overhead lifting machine.

She was quite bluff at the bows and now it was easier to read the parched paintwork on the piece of plywood at the port rail. It indicated $2500.00 so in reality Sam had already reduced the price, a reflection of the lack of care put to this sorry looking craft.

'If you haven't got any immediate questions I'll let you two have a bit of time to yourselves. If you want to go aboard, clear it with the foreman first, he'll get you a ladder, but tread softly when you're up there ok?'...

Sam wandered back to the café and as I watched him drifting away I couldn't help but sense that he was really just a little embarrassed at the state of the boat.

'Grace' was a sloop of some 8 metres . Looking up I could see that the aluminum mast and rigging was tired looking and unkempt.

The coach roof and presumably the deck was covered in mildew and seagull mess. The hull I gave greater attention to, as I was drawn to some ill fitting planks some open at the joints, making me think naturally of the frames inside. Her overall length was impressive enough, it didn't bother us that this was a hull not designed for speed bur for strength and longevity. The smile was slowly disappearing from my girl's face and then we both noticed at the same time that the iron keel appeared to be separating itself away from the timbers.

There was also plenty of rust around the rudder fittings.

We walked around and around several times, not quite sure what to do when the chap who had just scrubbed Grace's bottom came over carrying a decent ladder.

'The hatch is unlocked so you can take a peek inside, but tread carefully ok?.

We put the ladder in position tucking it against one of the port stanchions and wedged on the slipway.

'The guy said, 'Unless we hear from Sam, then we'll float her back to her mooring at six pm tonight. I'll be down here clearing up, shout if you need anything'..

There was only a gradual slope on the old slipway and because Grace's keel had a forward upward slope we soon discovered that topside all was fairly level to move safely around.

We stepped over the lifeline and settled into the cockpit, saddened at the grease and mildew everywhere, not forgetting the pidgeon

and seagull mess. I cast a gaze at Melanie –
'Maybe easier to buy an airline ticket?'.

She laughed as only she could and slid the main
hatch forward then removed the washboards,
carefully placing them next to me in the cockpit.
In two seconds she was down the
companionway steps and inside. She was keen.

I was strangely nervous but ventured
down behind her. It didn't take very long to
examine everything that was important to us
from a survival point of view. Yes, there were
some frame rot problems which were fixable
and some much needed upgrading required.

On the comfort side of things there was a
V berth in the forepeak cabin, and a chain locker
forward of that.

There were two saloon berths port and
starboard, with lee cloths that had seen better
days, rotting away beneath ageing and stained
seat cushions. Were it not for the ventilators in
the coach roof this boat would have smelled a
lot worse that was for sure. Melanie was deeply
into studying the 'galley'-basically a couple of
lockers, two small overhead cabinets and a

gimbaled cooker working from a gas bottle somewhere. I somehow knew what that would look like once I had located it in the cockpit locker. It was there, rusted and dangerous looking, along with the spider webs.

I couldn't imagine when somebody had last cooked a breakfast on the Lady Grace.
Although sparse, dirty and neglected, overall the interior was no worse nor better than what I had imagined and could be tidied up and the cosmetics improved.

She carried nearly a foot of water in the main bilge which I put down to plank and keel fastenings, but these things could be addressed.
The small diesel engine would need to be serviced and new bilge pumps installed as I doubt this vessel had ever travelled too far from her anchorage and things like electric bilge pumps tend to seize up and become unreliable.

We could both see the possibilities here, but there would be money involved.
'Melanie', I said, 'we would have to lay this boat up in the yard for a few weeks, maybe months-

just to make her seaworthy do you realize that?'.

She smiled as only she could, 'Yes, so what is the problem. This is an opportunity Phil, it means I can stay on at my job and half of the money that I earn can go towards the work. You can leave your hotel and I can stop paying rent. We could live onboard together, this will be our new home!'...

As soon as she said this, my interest in the boat was re-ignited, my doubts turned into promises and a new commitment.

'By golly I think you've got something honey, after all what's the point in panicking. Time is on our side!'.

We sat back in the filthy cockpit, both imagining how perfect the Lady Grace could look with some time and patience.

After a quick look at the decrepit standing and running rigging on deck I said 'come on, let's go and find Sam'.

We thanked the foreman as he took the ladder away, and five minutes later we found Sam in his usual location still looking a little tense, but understandable in the circumstances.

Morning had long turned to afternoon as we sat down next to him, just a few people dotted around but the odour of cooked food wafting from the café reminded me that we'd missed lunch.

'Another coffee Sam?'

Breaking into a rare smile he said, 'Don't worry it's on the way young man, along with some sandwiches, I expect you're hungry'.

It seemed to me that Sam wanted to keep us there for as long as possible to work on a deal somehow and his efforts were not going unnoticed but on the contrary, they were appreciated.

We talked openly about our plans and how Melanie and I could live on the Grace whilst getting her shipshape. This made a lot of sense to us as the money saved in not paying rent could be put into expenses on board.

I was gazing at Sam, he was gently rubbing his chin and acknowledging the arrival of the coffee and food.

I said, 'Considering how much work we would have to put into her and make her seaworthy, what's your best discount price?'.

He stroked his chin a little more and sipped his coffee, 'Tell you what, I'm happy to eat the cost of the haul out and the bottom scrub as I figure that's down to me anyway, but I won't budge lower than $1800. But if you agree, Grace will have to be moved back into the yard to a suitable spot to store her, which is your cost. The haul out cost me $200, I figure they'll charge you a hundred dollars to relocate her to a position where you can both live and work on her'.

The immediate thought of $1900 and a total life changing experience was a little bit intimidating but as I caught Melanie's smiling glance I knew that she was in for the challenge.

Sam was quick to remind us that until we could cook onboard, there was the café for meals at a moment's notice!..

I leaned forward, satisfied at the outcome and shook his hand, 'It's a deal Sam, thank you'.

No sooner had the cheese and tomato sandwiches been consumed, when Sam stretched to his feet.

'Ok, I must report to the yard office and change their plans before the tide comes too close. It's time to move your boat you guys!'...

Now that the deal was struck it was time to watch Grace being lifted through the yard to a quiet spot away from the main boatyard activities

She was set on blocks, shores in place and plenty of space around her in which to work and organize.

Behind Grace was a fenced field of barley stretching into the distance forming a sweet backdrop to this place where the land meets the sea.

I put my arm around her shoulder, she slipped her arm around my waist, 'This is our new home, or at least it will be soon I hope!'

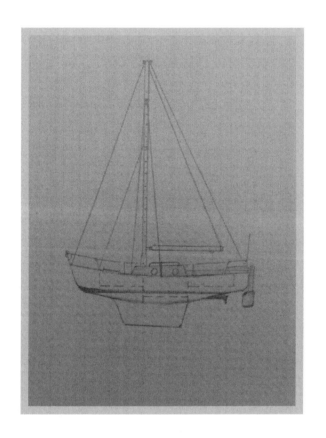

Lady Grace

.CHAPTER THREE

I signed out of the hotel and temporarily moved in with Melanie at her small flat.

There was urgent work to do on Grace to enable us to move onboard in relative comfort. It would take me at least two weeks to create a safe galley and clean out the bilges to get rid of the terrible damp smell.

There was plenty to do and I reckoned three weeks before we could move onboard and feel fairly comfortable with our surroundings.

Early October 1995, and without the hire car most of our running around was done using Melanie's motor scooter.

Whilst she was busy at her day job, I would ferret around gathering tools and equipment needed to start on these early projects which would lead to our new habitation. I tackled the bilges first, considering this to be most important not just because of the smell, but to allow everything below the cabin sole level to dry out. It was when cleaning the bilge near the stern that I discovered the build year etched into timbers, 1955!- with the name of the builder also half corroded away onto a small zinc label.

I had been correct in my assumption of Grace's forty years!.

After each hard day's work, I would hurry back to my fiancee's flat and we would have a well earned dinner and rest. Things were moving on.

Within a week, Melanie was very sad one night explaining that in a couple of days she would have to say goodbye to three of her favorite and best friends.

The Sea life Centre were releasing three dolphins back into the ocean where hopefully they would someday breed and enjoy their new found freedom.

Feeding them on a daily basis and training them to do various simple tasks had brought a special bonding that she was sad to be losing. Much quieter than normal, she did ask me to be present with her at the time of their release.

It was something that I had never experienced before on that Friday afternoon at the poolside of the dolphins.

Only the few staff were there as they had closed the facility for the afternoon.

Melanie had brought their final meal of fresh herrings, and laying down at the edge of the pool she fed, kissed and patted each of their sweet snouts, talking to them and saying their final goodbyes. I was totally dumbstruck and choked up to see the level of bonding, never even gave a thought to the obvious conversation of dolphins.

It was really moving when suddenly Melanie, wearing her black one piece swimsuit jumped to her feet and waved her arms into the air in the shape of a large arc. The three dolphins exploded into a lap of the pool then created a huge jump exactly in the centre.

The sluice gate was immediately raised at the ocean wall and the grateful, graceful mammals although reluctantly at first, soon disappeared into the green blue depths beyond.

All three dolphins were tagged on their dorsal fins and Max, the male and largest, led the way closely followed by Anna the female. The smallest was Daisy, at only two metres, she took a little longer before committing.

Melanie was down on her knees at the pool's edge and I held her shoulder as she looked up at me, tears weeping from her eyes.

Sam had now been paid for the Lady Grace and we had a monthly ground fee to pay to the boatyard. Melanie and I had decided that it was pointless for her to give up her job as we needed the income and so therefore we would stick to the plan and become a working team at weekends and her odd days off from the Sea Life Centre.

The arrangement suited us both and in a couple of weeks we would be able to vacate the small flat and strike a saving there.

Grace's location at the back of the boatyard was idyllic really, away from the noise and dust of the other boat owners. She was well propped up onto good firm soil and blocked under her keel.

With the interior more or less stripped back to bulkheads and berths, it was like having a blank canvas to start afresh!. In two weeks I had to create enough comfort to welcome my girl onboard for good. I had my work cut out.

I would often stand outside, walk around Grace, longing for that stage of her restoration, to make her look shipshape and beautiful again. But for now my efforts had to be on her interior or at least as much as was possible.

Sam would occasionally drop by out of interest and was a useful mind of information regarding tracking down bits and pieces in our quest to getting the boat seaworthy again.

In a week the bilges were drying out nicely and the bulkheads were cleaned down and freshly painted. I've always likened the smell of new paint which gives encouragement and a sense of progress.

I made new paper templates for all the berth and bunk cushions and took these to an upholsterer just a mile away to have new replacements made.

Before I could think about the galley I was concerned about the keel bolts, something that could not be ignored considering the age of the boat. The bolt heads over the keel plate in the bilge told me that it was worth investigating, I certainly don't like rust on a boat. The iron keel itself didn't fit too well on the outside, there was clearly movement or had been in the past. I continually soaked the bolt heads with penetrating fluid for two days whilst doing other work, before attempting to loosen them.

I had to do the same on the outside, tracking the positions of the relevant galleries, the location holes where there would be nuts and washers to access. This involved chopping away all the filler and paint that had been crammed into the galleries, over the wooden plugs fitted there to protect the nuts and bolts from the elements.

The last thing I wanted to do was remove or even lower the keel but, peace of mind was uppermost in my thoughts and a long term view to selling the boat once Melanie and I had settled back in Sydney.

Of the ten keel bolts to give attention to, only four was I able to loosen and withdraw as the penetration fluid had done its job and seeped down through to the nuts and washers.

With all of the galleries exposed and cleared out on the outside, I could make a plan.

The remaining six bolts had either broken or were now spinning continuously into their respective nuts indicating that rust had rotted the threads. Using one of the good bolts as a template I was able to purchase all new bolts and so began the tiresome task of extracting the bad bolts, cutting into the nuts at the galleries with an air saw and eventually removing the folding wedges under the keel and lowering it just enough to allow cleaning of the joint and applying new sealing putty.

With the hull well supported and braced I was able to complete the whole job, new bolts installed and tightened, and the keel wedged up again tight and true, in three days but I was exhausted in the process.

With Grace now sitting firmly on her keel again and a smug look upon my face, I had three working days prior to Melanie moving onboard, which meant only one thing...the galley!

A final tighten on the keel bolt heads and down went the sole boards at last.
Now I could work on board and foresee some progress.
Scrambling around in the cockpit lockers was painful, so much cleaning to do and then make a new gas bottle stowage with a new supply line through the bulkhead and to the awaiting cooker.
There were two main bilge pumps, one operating from the cockpit to the bilge area beneath the diesel engine, and one mounted near the small chart table beneath the starboard berth, serving the saloon bilge area. I made a point of making sure that the bilge area was clear right through the boat.

Both of these pumps exited through the hull above the water line. I took these pumps apart and was lucky enough to be able to buy new diaphragms from the yard store and a couple of extra ones for spares.

Knowing that the bilges were clean and not clogged up with rubbish was a good feeling. Having two good manual bilge pump's was an even better feeling.

But I did promise myself after advice from Sam, that I would fit an electric automatic pump to the main bilge as a safeguard.

Melanie was able to start helping out where she could and cleaned up the cooker with a lot of effort. Although looking like a relic from a 1950's café, it was now gleaming.

The really good thing was that it actually worked and justified the cost of a new gas bottle and fittings.

It had to be said that although things were coming together, the interior was quite depressing without any upholstery and the anticipated delivery on the coming Saturday couldn't come quick enough for us.

Money was not an immediate problem but with Melanie still working it added to the stability of the situation.

With 24 hours before vacating her flat, the reality of our commitment started to sink in, then a fresh wave of excitement welled up inside me as I realized that we were half way into our new adventure.

Soon we would have blue water under our keel and a dream for the future.

After the weekend I knew that I would be transferring my activities to the outside, working on the hull.

New Zealand's summer was nigh and occasionally we would wander down to the water's edge and sit there for a while, contemplating our unfolding story. In a way we both felt privileged to be living this opportunity of a new dream.

As we gazed out beyond the anchorage Melanie said, 'I miss my friend's and I hope that they're safe now especially Anna and Daisy, they will have a lot to learn to survive'.

I'd completely forgotten how deep her attachment to the dolphins had been and how much she cared about those two females especially. Max, the larger male would no doubt have taken an independent strike out for total freedom, though there was a chance according to Melanie that all three may have stuck together for security until they would have met up with larger social groups, always on the hunt for food.

But with Lady Grace's demands upon us, we pressed on. We clambered up onto her deck and slid the already disconnected mast down onto the ground so that it could be carried to the workshop for an overhaul.

After that, we locked Grace up for the evening and retired to the flat for one Last time and to pack our stuff ready for Saturday's transition.

It was early November 1995.

After a month of activity since purchasing Grace, the days were getting warmer as springtime advanced, and we were comfortable on board. Repairing the hull's planks, caulking and sanding had taken its toll on me and I was so glad that applying new paint was not far away, the weather permitting.

I'd enlisted the help of a boat builder just to repair the rudder and fit new gudgeons to the transom and pintle's to the repaired blade. The tiller was also none the good for wear and I struck a deal with the chap to make a replacement from solid teak, easy enough from the many scraps found inside the boat shed.

Melanie was still employed at the Sea Life Centre and our transition to onboard living had not been so drastic as I had feared.

We always had a cooked meal together in the evenings onboard, sometimes nipping over to the café for a break in routine.

We also took breakfast there at least twice a week.

By the end of November the hull was fully painted, red below the waterline and white on the topsides. Not a pristine job, but a very tidy one, and much better than her previous state.

The rudder was fixed and re-hung and I turned my attention to the deck and cockpit, a grim task as the deck planking was in poor shape but too far out of reach financially to consider re-planking.

I decided on simply caulking the joints, sanding down, and making sure that all was weather tight and presentable.

Towards the end of November and with our fresh sun tans growing, a full two weeks had passed by and the deck was acceptable and the cockpit was scrubbed clean and shipshape. I had fitted new fastenings to all of the deck cleats just for good measure, a small expense for greater reliability. That old saying came to mind, don't spoil the ship for a halfpenny worth' of tar!

The more we advanced into December it became obvious that our departure this side of

Christmas was unrealistic.

Thankfully it was comfortable on board, and we were happy just to take our time knowing that summer was on the horizon.

Whilst the mast and rigging were being overhauled I rented some floor space at the local sail makers. Their loft floor was just what we needed to lay the sails out and inspect for damage. Lady Grace didn't boast a choice of sail options.

The mainsail was fairly old but, being terylene was in pretty good shape and only needed some running eyes replacing.

There were two jibs of different sizes and one genoa. The jibs were cotton canvas I suspect original, but in reasonable shape. The genoa like the main, needed some attention.

But it was good to lay them all out one at a time and have the sail maker undertake the necessary repairs including some re-stitching of the seams. This 'hospital' job I left to the guy in charge of the business who at this time of year had little else to keep him busy. The good thing was that it freed me up to concentrate on the hardcore of Grace's endless list of jobs to carry out.

One evening after dinner I realized that a trip to Auckland was necessary to renew my already extended holiday visa at the Australian Embassy.

This would entail a two day 450 mile round trip, far too much for the scooter and so we decided that this would be our last duty to perform in December. Once that was done we would ease back a bit prior to Christmas. In the New Year we would pick up the pieces after re-charging our batteries so to speak. Melanie and I both needed a rest for a while.

The trip by train to Auckland we both enjoyed so much and it was a huge relief to extend my visa. After that, Christmas 1995 was fairly quiet with occasional trips into town to visit friends' of Melanie's or have lunch somewhere warm and friendly and escape the chore of cooking onboard.

We toasted the New Year in gazing out over the harbour and Melanie raised a glass of wine to celebrate her dolphin friends' new found freedom. She would never forget them that was for sure.

There was still several weeks of the summer period left to finalize our preparations and I felt sure I would need to keep an eye on my bank account as it seemed that every other day there was something that had to be bought and paid for other than for food and yard rental.

It was time to keep a slight reign on the expenses, and make a final list of jobs to do.

Being outside was best, just shorts and T shirts, clambering around up on deck and messing about around the boat painting fixtures and fittings.

This was New Zealand's summer period and we made the most of the good dry weather which would run through until the end of February, to complete all of the outside jobs that we could think of. We figured that a sensible target for re-launching the boat would be the end of January to the middle of February. There was a twinge of excitement at the prospect of that happening.

Sam came by one morning with news that somebody local was selling their ship to shore radio for a modest fifty dollars and I eagerly snapped this up, a cash gift from my fiancee!, and within 24 hours it was fitted onto the chart table bulkhead and wired up to our domestic battery. This one item of equipment made me feel a whole lot better about our journey where safety had to be paramount.

The engine start battery was located safely under the chart table seat, and the engine start switch was mounted inside the cockpit coaming to help keep it dry, away from the elements in bad weather.

Although the small 10 hp diesel would start, we couldn't really run it for too long without connecting a water supply up into the heat exchanger unit which was mounted ahead of the engine on the bulkhead. This was something I would have to address later when we were afloat either in the dock or upon Grace's mooring. I figured we would live afloat there for two to three days whilst preparing for our departure.

The cabin electrics checked out ok and the radio tested good on a test call to the local coastguard.

Both batteries were connected to the engine alternator so that hopefully if the batteries ran down, we could recharge them. Everything here was going to be a challenge, certainly the largest challenge of my life but, like all journey's in life, it is the preparation that would lead to success. After that we are all in God's hands.

CHAPTER FOUR

By mid February we had achieved almost everything that our jobs to do list had dictated.

Plenty of provisions like canned food and drinking water were stored onboard under the saloon and forward berths.

The mast and rigging had been overhauled and the bill paid. The weather was still quite warm and only moderate breezes coming from the west on most days.

With mounting nervous excitement we committed to have Grace moved to the dock on the 17th February where her mast would be re-stepped and secured to the tabernacle, her overhauled standing rigging reset and secured.

It left me two or three days to find a couple of decent life jackets and a small life raft if at all possible. We were lucky on both counts at the chandlery store on site and for a moderate cost our preparations were nearly complete. I found myself almost constantly looking at the sky, the young sailor in me urging to escape.

It was the 20th February and Grace was proudly swinging back on her mooring where a few months before, she looked a very sad case in need of some real help.

The life raft was lashed to chocks on the cabin coach roof and the electrics on the mast checked out with all the navigation lights working.

The engine had been run up in the dock by a yard engineer and all had checked out ok, a new filter put into the water input strainer just for good measure. Melanie reminded me to buy spare fuel, something that had almost been forgotten.

That evening we rowed ashore in the dinghy to have dinner at the cafe with Sam, who was just as excited as we were of our impending departure. He very graciously handed the dinghy to us as a gift and in a way it provided further comfort to us as a safety measure and a convenience for the future.

It was only a small fibre glass boat of some eight

feet in length, but would easily be towed behind Grace, leaving precious deck space free for both of us to move around.

The three of us tucked into a beef stew followed by fruit and wine, the sun starting to settle to the west bringing a warm, soft halo settling around the horizon.

'So when's the big day for the big 'off' you two?'—
I said, 'Well, I think we've decided on the 23rd which is a Friday, a much more pleasant sounding day than a Monday!'.
Sam smiled, and complimented us on what looked like a job well done with Grace looking so well presented on her mooring in the near distance, her white topsides glistening with the watery reflections.

'You'll find that the cockpit compass is a good one, what other navigational aids do you have ?' he said, peering over his wine glass.

I said, 'Well, we have good charts, the radio and such like, but no fancy sat nav back up like all these modern sailors, what do you think?'..He paused to think a little, swallowed some food, breathed a contented sigh, 'Well, you have a five day minimum journey, maybe more depending on the wind and the currents.

The secret will be to stay on course and allow for the tidal drift. If it were me, I would get a sat nav receiver just for peace of mind, it would help you to check your position at any time, it would be an extra string to your bow, best to be covered you know?'

Melanie glanced at me and straight away I knew that Sam was right. I had always pushed this item to the back of my mind because of the expense involved, but in truth without it Grace could be a loose pebble bouncing on the waves of doubt in my mind and I had Melanie to think about now, we were a couple and common sense had to prevail.

I really had not enough long distance sailing experience to put our lives at risk unnecessarily.

So, once again the next day we found ourselves at the chandlery store at the boatyard checking the items for sale on the signboard in the window. The man inside gave us a wave and beckoned us inside. I didn't relish spending yet more money but we wandered inside anyway. We had come to regard Robert as a friend and he could detect our concern.

'I take it you'll be leaving us soon, so this could be your last chance to do some shopping?'I told him of our desire to have a satellite navigation aid, nothing too fancy but in good working order.

'Then you've come to the right place once again my boy, follow me!'..
He led us to the store room at the rear and said, 'I know you probably can't afford a new unit but',--he waved his hands invitingly at a shelf full of second hand goods.

'Where there's a will!'—
We were quite surprised at the stuff spread before us, and a choice of at least five good sat nav receivers, probably trade in's or rescued gear from dismantled craft.

A huge grin came upon my face and it wasn't long before we'd settled on a choice, plus lots of good advice from Robert on how to install the unit.

'It might take you a day to run your power lines and fit your aerial to your push pit or maybe the masthead but either way, all this stuff here works'.

We settled on two hundred dollars which left a dent in my wallet but was much better than forking out $1000 for a new unit!.

We reckoned that our purchase was probably five years old, but was in good, clean condition.

I was looking forward to installing it onto the Lady Grace.

CHAPTER FIVE

It was Saturday 24th February and we were both a little nervous yet excited to embark on our new adventure.

We had used up an extra day to complete installing the sat nav receiver which was mounted immediately above the starboard chart table onto the bulkhead above. I had fastened the small dish aerial to the starboard side of the push pit which made it relatively easy to route the cable from that to the unit inside the cabin.

We were both fairly familiar with the rig now, having enjoyed the repair and re-fit process.

With a hug from Melanie I started the engine, leaving it to idle while we set the jib half out but not tight. The main was reefed to the boom ready for use at a later time.

We both waved to the café and Sam and a few others were there waving back to us.

That was when I felt the real adrenaline rush and got the urge to shed a small tear.

With Melanie at the tiller I went forward and prepared to let go of the mooring warp.

With a nod from me, she throttled forward a little to release the tension and gave me the vocal message I needed –'Ok, release'.
I let the warp fall away free and Grace slowly moved forward .

I headed back to the cockpit to take the tiller and hold my place alongside my fiancee. We kept on waving and headed for the harbour entrance on the outgoing tide, just starting to ebb now. Our journey had begun.
With Grace moving under mostly engine power, for the first time I could feel the true weight of our vessel, our home.
She slipped down the channel with a definite direction and ease of handling and I only hoped that she would be equally responsive under sail.

It was 1.00 pm and we would have four to five hours of sunshine before a sunset would beckon us on westward.

With the harbor entrance falling away behind us, Grace slid into her motion dipping through the slight swell and I could feel and see the sudden change of depth of water from a sweet pale yellow, to a deeper green with blue to follow.

We set a course slightly north of west and I went forward to set the jib.

Grace heeled to port, sucking in the extra power from the jib, sucking in the North Westerly breeze with almost grateful glee.

I decided not to raise the main until we had both got used to handling the boat a bit more but in good time we would have to in order to make good steerage and headway.

Melanie brought sandwiches from the galley and we both sat back in the cockpit taking in the view of our surrounding splendor. Only the noisy sounds of the following gulls looking for scraps to keep us company.

I had logged our departure with the local coastguard prior to leaving and all there was now to do was cut the engine and see how Grace picked up under sail.

She was not a lightweight, I reckoned close to four tons including her long iron keel. Everything now was a learning curve for both of us, which was part of the excitement and fun.

Melanie held the course whilst I winched the main two thirds up, made fast the halyard and tightened the main sheet at the cockpit. She instantly heeled another five degrees and picked up another two knots of speed. We were hoping to average about five knots generally, given that we had good wind.

Still, the boat was comfortable even with a fair lean on. We had a good three feet of freeboard at near the cockpit which was good but in no way did I ever want to try dipping the toe rail with a boat like Grace. She was not a performance vessel, merely a workhorse, a mule of the sea's that needed respect and treating kindly.

We were probably making a good four knots by my judgment and towing our small dinghy some ten feet behind, still with sail power to spare if needed.

We also had the genoa, newly repaired and ready to use if we needed but for now stowed in the forward cabin. Therefore I felt quite comfortable in our situation as the mainland coastline disappeared in a haze behind us. Now all we had to do was enjoy the experience.

The feel of the wooden deck below my feet was wonderful as Melanie cried excitedly across the cockpit, 'Look, Look',--

I climbed into the cockpit beside her and she pointed at the waves beyond some 100 feet. Three to four large dolphins broke the surface and charged on ahead as often they do, playing games and making a pace.

They were much faster than Grace could ever be but it was nice to share the seas with such creatures. Melanie was standing up searching the horizon, a sad look on her face.

'What's wrong honey?'
'Oh, it's just that I realize that I've lost my babies you know, I wonder every day where can they be and I worry about Daisy especially'.

I really felt for her, 'Don't worry they can look after themselves and you can always work with dolphins again in Sydney you know?'.
She smiled again and sat back into the cockpit hugging the tiller, still scanning the horizon left to right, far and wide.

We managed to stay on our present course but because we didn't have auto pilot, we had to take watches, always one of us at the tiller even if it was lashed amidships. This meant that we were sleeping alone, always one of us on lookout from the cockpit and the other snatching what little sleep we could afford. This had worked well for three days.

Tuesday 27th February, it was midday, and I realized that we were drifting further north than anticipated according to our sat nav. I corrected the course more to a westerly point to counteract the tidal drift and would see how we would fare staying on the port tack.

Grace was still making my estimate of four to five knots of speed even though the seas were getting choppier, and just a little bit more uncomfortable.

This was causing the dinghy to slam hard in the wake, the tow line jerking violently to the stern cleat but we pushed on.

With a deeply graying sky around 1.00 pm, Melanie had just made coffee and was bringing it up to the cockpit when I looked into the near distance and caught sight of something I didn't like.

An enormous squall, black and heavy looking, dead ahead. I took a sip of coffee and felt the instant sharp breeze hit my face, coming straight at us, the forbearer of the oncoming danger. Melanie looked anxiously at me,

'What's wrong Phil?'..

I quickly swallowed my drink and tossed the cup down into the galley.

'We have to reduce the main quickly, that ahead doesn't look too good, no time to waste!'

She checked my line of sight, seeing the sky slowly turning black and threatening, the halyards starting to rattle alarmingly.

'What do we do Phil?'

'Sit tight and I'll reef the main in some or we could get damage. I reckon we have five minutes before it'll swamp us and let's hope it doesn't last too long!'

I knew that getting caught unprepared in a large squall could be very dangerous, and already Grace was butting madly into the ever enlarging oncoming waves. The sky was quickly not just turning black but very intimidating and hostile.

At least we were facing the oncoming maelstrom.

Our speed of course was suffering and all we could do was point Grace straight into the sharply increasing wind which was now slapping madly at the jib and tearing into our eyes.

The booming of the dinghy tow line had me worried as I feared the possibility of losing our little friend. If it broke loose, we had no chance of recovering it in rough conditions.

My fears rose to the surface within two minutes as a sudden wind tempest threw itself upon us with immense driving rain.

Grace rose and pitched uncomfortably, as the horizon all around seemed to disappear within seconds. I reached into the port cockpit locker to grab our lifejackets. 'Here, put this on just in case, don't worry, we'll be ok!'

I knew that Melanie was a very strong swimmer but this was no time to be a dreamer.

We just had time to tighten our lifejackets and I secured the reefing on the boom, almost falling twice against the rising and pitching cockpit.

We both clung to the tiller and hoped to good luck that all would be fine. I could see that Melanie was anxious and tried to reassure her, keeping my own thoughts to myself. I had sailed through squalls before but nothing like this, not on this scale. I began to wish that Grace was a hundred feet longer or that by design we could simply maneuver around this storm but it was far too big, monstrously wide and the shrieking wind was getting stronger every second that passed.

The black sky joined up with the rising sea which seemed even blacker as the white contrasting bow waves from the pounding hull, seemed to take off and saturate us back in the cockpit.

This was going to test Grace's fifty year old hull to the maximum and I admit I felt just a little sceptical as more and more of what was left of the blue sky simply vanished and we became surrounded now by the unforgiving darkness, and crashing of the wind all around.

Melanie kept staring back at the dinghy. She could hardly hear me as I shouted,'Don't worry, if we lose it we lose it. There's nothing we can do!'.

I jumped to the port winch to tighten the jib as it was trying to thrash itself free, taking an extra turn and cleating it fast for good measure and then falling back beside Melanie who by now was beginning to look more than scared.

I placed a reassuring arm around her shoulder, the tiller jammed between our rain and spray soaked bodies.

CHAPTER SIX

It seemed like Grace was almost stationary and it was certainly impossible to detect a forward motion as we crashed violently into the oncoming wave surge for at least another hour and it felt like a lifetime until the rain ceased and the black clouds gave way to the oncoming dusk, and a welcome fresh breeze ensued.

I looked ahead, yes evening was nigh but checking our position was important.
I climbed down into the cabin and switched on the sat nav only to find after the screen lit up that it quickly switched off again.

My heart sank as I tried repeatedly to fire it up but to no avail.
Melanie glanced inside at me, sensing my frustration. I looked at the control panel eager to see the battery charge indicator.

It showed no power, how could this be?-
Dusk was about to fall on us and we had to at the very least, run our navigation lights. Either we had inherited a duff battery or the engine

alternator was not functioning properly.

'Melanie,-start the engine quickly but don't engage drive, we need battery power.' My mind was in a daze when she switched on and turned the key. The engine starter motor chugged around very slowly, grinding to a lazy halt, telling me that despite running the engine on our first day for maybe four hours to charge the batteries, they had completely run down without warning since then.

Now the engine wouldn't fire up, the batteries were sucked dry.   We'd had the alternator serviced and checked. Grace was still pitching and rolling and the thought of crawling down through the locker to spread myself around the engine and attempt to investigate the problem was a daunting task but I had to do it.

'Hold on honey', I shouted as I grabbed my small tool bag and lifted the locker lid. We were still riding four foot waves and a deep swell. Grace took another pitch and I almost fell into the locker head first. The creaking sounds coming from the wooden hull were not sweet as

I could sense how hard this storm was affecting her integrity. Deep inside I hoped that the hull itself had not been compromised in any way.

I checked all the connections and all seemed well. Grace rolled again and I banged my head on the underside of the cockpit floor.
I had no volt meter and very few electrical tools to check for continuity or a live circuit. In all honesty electricity was not one of my strong points in life. I preferred a liking to things I could see rather than could not.

Fighting my anger and frustration I turned myself around and groped my way back up into the cockpit. My ribs ached and I felt exhausted, slightly nauseous and sick of the motion crawling around the diesel engine.

I rejoined Melanie, not being able to hide my anxiety, but she seemed to know that we had a real problem.
It was getting darker now. Grace plunged on through the swell, the jib and main trimmed back, but probably only making about three to four knots until I could make sail adjustments.

Instinctively I climbed into the cabin and

reached at the radio above the chart table. I was still soaking wet and feeling downtrodden.

My worst fears soon were realized when I switched on the radio. The operation light instantly faded to darkness and I cursed the $50 dollar unit that had no provision for DC batteries. What was I thinking?—
Without onboard electrical power we were desperate, or at least at night we were.

No radio, no navigation lights, and no sat nav. I climbed back to the tiller, 'Melanie, make some coffee honey would you, I'll keep our course and soon we'll get some more sail up but for now, I need some strong coffee. Go careful down the steps'. I was scared of falling asleep.

She nodded at me and skipped down to the galley. I sat back clutching the tiller, and constantly checking the compass.
We were in a mess and the sense of adventure had quickly degenerated into one of extreme concern. I had to think. The diesel engine had no hand crank facility.
With night blanketing down around us and the plunge of the swell annoying me I decided that

the only positive thing to do was increase our sail power in the hope of shortening our journey. It would be better than chopping up and down relentlessly with hardly any forward motion.

I quickly released the reefs on the boom and hoisted the main as much as I dared and made it fast again.

Instantly Grace smacked over as she caught the extra wind which put us on a starboard tack. The ever tricky wind had now come round from the south catching me unprepared. Stepping back into the cockpit I slackened the main sheet to let the boom go a bit, release us from the sudden force and the crazy angle.

I swear the rail was nearly under, something I wouldn't do unless I was racing a dinghy. But this was Grace, fifty years old and a vague history of her sailing days. It was 7.00pm.We had certainly picked up some extra speed to which I reckoned now must have been six to seven knots but it wasn't comfortable to say the least. The jib was still straining and I realized that the wind was on the up again.

I didn't like being on this starboard tack but we had to make some serious headway if possible.

With disappearing light the very thought of being stranded out here in the night without any navigation lights or engine power was almost too shameful to contemplate, and now the seas were getting much choppier again.

Melanie struggled up the companionway steps and handed me the coffee. It was 10.00 pm. Exhausted from the hard ride, I said to her, 'Watch the compass honey, I'm going below to check the wiring at the batteries, I may have missed something you never know!'.

Grace was still pounding into the rough, chopping swells, the boom swung out some 10 degrees on the lee side to somewhat lessen the strain on the rig.

We still had the compass heading of slightly north of west. There was no moon, but blackness all around. That's one thing I don't like. I passed one of our flashlights out to Melanie to help her keep an eye on the compass which although having a fluorescent bezel, was rather faint from a distance.

The other flashlight was stronger and using this, I was able to grope around in the cabin checking wiring and lifting sole boards.

In the dark, creaking interior I could see and hear some water washing around in the bilge. I wasn't surprised at this considering how many breakers had swept over the cockpit.

I put the sole boards back in place, not wanting to deviate from the electrical problem. I had a job to stand up with Grace heeling and plunging on her present heel of angle.

I glanced out to Melanie who was still pre-occupied with the dinghy tow line tension and was leaning over pushpit rail trying to fasten an extra line to act as a spring coil. I called to her not to worry though I doubt that she could hear me properly through the screeching southerly din. The noise was frightening to be truthful.

I ducked back down to continue my check on the battery connections and after a short while and starting to feel nauseous again I came up for air. When I next looked into the cockpit Melanie wasn't there.

I stared at the empty space next to the tiller. My disbelieving senses told me that she must have gone forward on the side deck for some reason.

I called her name and lunged upwards into the windswept cockpit, my head turning immediately to look forward to the mast and the foredeck expecting her to be there but no, she was nowhere to be seen.

I screamed her name into the blackness over and over again, saw her flashlight rolling around in the water drenched cockpit.
Never had I felt so terrified. Not for me, but for my sweet Melanie. There was no other in my life.

Two distraught minutes must have passed in the blackness before I realized that the tow line to the dinghy was gone, a small tether still wrapped around the cleat where it must have snapped.

I sunk to my knees in despair still shouting her name, to see the horizon would have been some comfort but to find her in the darkness with no moon and a chaotic rising storm seemed impossible. I wasn't worried about the dinghy, that was superfluous, though a glimmer of hope told me that she may have managed to get to it, if it had not already been sunk or compromised by the heavy sea.

There was nothing to do but drop the mainsail again if I could and try to come about, try for a random search in the darkness but because the southern wind was so strong, making it back around to where she must have gone overboard was not going to be easy.

But I had to try in my desperation.

'God help us'-I kept repeating to myself as I attempted to reef the main once again, the wind tearing at my face. Knowing that my next move was to turn Grace with the wind in order to get some momentum and double back was playing on my mind. This could be dangerous. I was praying that Melanie was still conscious and that her lifejacket was doing its job.

With the main well reefed I released the lashing to the tiller and easing in on the main sheet a little, I turned her to starboard, Grace suddenly running with the wind across the waves in a northerly direction. I counted to five, and swung to starboard again, the boom flying over my head and checking above the port side deck.

In my mind I was heading back to Melanie's probable location but with the wind and the sea state working against me I was cursing the unpredictable conditions that had changed our journey of discovery into one of a nightmare in the truest sense of the word.

I had to save her.

What I would have given for a clear sky and a bright moon, how different things could be.

Grace cruised awkwardly onward, dipping and groaning, the jib once again was flapping madly as it struggled to contain the velocity of this mad southerly. I swear it was turning into a tempest.

CHAPTER SEVEN

Quickly lashing the tiller again I scrambled to locate the flashlight swimming around in the cockpit. It still worked thank God!

If I could find her or the dinghy, it would be a miracle I knew that but I had to try.

Down in the saloon things were starting to break loose and fall around. I waved the flashlight beam madly into the oncoming gloom screaming her name as I went, praying for her very soul.

After ten minutes of hanging on for dear life, I turned Grace into the wind, pointing southwards, wallowing sideways against the mighty chop, and so therefore completing an imaginary circle of a search pattern. The boom swung back to midships but I was ready for it and ducked in time to re-lash the tiller to keep us into the onslaught. This was frantic stuff, but I was trying to keep a cool head.

I kept flashing the beam all around and shouting out for her. She may have been doing the same thing for all I know, but I would never have heard her voice being drowned out by the wind and the ocean in its fury.

I knew that the waters here were quite cold having swept up from the Arctic Circle and there was a ton of latitude to creep north before the waters became warmer. Without the dinghy, she wouldn't survive for more than two or three hours in the water with just a lifejacket on. Hypothermia would soon take its inevitable toll upon her.

Glancing at the compass, it was turning crazily from one direction to another trying to keep up with Grace's movements.

'If only I could start the engine'.. kept running through my head, but sadly it was a doom laden wish that wasn't going to happen.

I was frantically hopping from port to starboard, shouting and waving the flashlight. Hanging on to the shrouds and the lifelines, I crept painfully along the side decks going forward, anything to somehow get a better view over the angry void before me 'Oh, dear God!' I glanced at my watch, 11.00pm –time was rushing by and I crept around to the starboard side deck hanging on for dear life like before and then found myself checking the security of the life raft lashed on chocks to the cabin roof. It was ok. Grace was now dipping and diving like a fishing trawler but it wasn't her fault.

I couldn't give her the attention she needed in the circumstances. But storms like this are unpredictable and arise from nowhere. This was how ships get lost completely in the Southern Ocean, there is always little warning.

Still shouting and waving the flashlight, I clambered back into the cockpit, a huge wave drenching me as I moved.

Grace rose up at the stern at the same time as my feet touched the cockpit floor, but the timing was not good and as I lost my balance, the last thing I remember was the boom snapping sideways at me and I fell against the main sheet loosing the downhaul out of the jam cleat.

As Grace swung violently to starboard, the boom was free to travel and I was helpless to avoid the oncoming collision like in a slow motion movie.

CHAPTER EIGHT

28th February 3.00am. My world was spinning into a black void or was it a dream?

Gradually the noises got much louder and my brain was trying to register these noises. Instinctively I looked at the grating that I was lying upon. Seas were crashing over me as I lay there and my watch was staring at me as the fearful crashing and banging intensified. The luminous face said 3.00am which made me snap into reality.

Rolling over onto my back in the pitching cockpit, the full horror of my situation reached up, slapped me in the face and awakened me. I was looking up at the black, ghostly side of an enormous ship moving quite fast and pushing onwards unaware of Grace smashing into the huge motoring hulk.

The skies were still dark but this ship was a terrifying dull giant and worst of all, Grace's mast was snapped at the spreaders, the top section hanging over the toe rail with halyards and rigging spread about the coach roof.

I tried to get up but it wasn't easy. The boat was being thrown and tossed like a cork, rising and crashing ten to fifteen feet at a time. I quickly assumed that the ship had run into us in the dark, my all time fear with having no navigation lights onboard.

Within a minute the grim silhouette of the great container ship was past me, cruising on into the darkness, oblivious of our plight below. Only the deep rumble of the mighty engines fading into the distance signaled its very existence, coupled with the odd cabin and deck light. I must have been unconscious for at least four hours and God alone knows where we had drifted to.

I had a throbbing head and a huge lump, seeping blood at my left temple. One thing was sure in the meantime, we had found the shipping lanes.

With my heart breaking I immediately thought of Melanie and what I could do next. The very thought of maybe finding her, albeit a slim one, drove me on to somehow get to grips with my situation and survive at all costs.

With Grace leaning at a crazy angle due to the rig hanging over the starboard rail there was nothing to do but brace myself and get to work.

I was completely soaking wet, still in just a T shirt and shorts, my feet slipping dangerously on the companionway steps as I tried to get below to find the hacksaw. Not unexpectedly, the floors were awash in seawater but that problem would have to wait for now.

Resisting the urge to be sick from the massive motions of the seaway, I climbed back up into the cold, shrieking wind, hacksaw in hand, and a spinning head.

One look at the damage and I knew that rescuing the damaged upper section would be a waste of time. It was mangled beyond recognition as a result of being continually smashed against the container ship's hull. All I could do was hopefully cut it away. I fastened a lifeline to my belt and back to the nearest stanchion. Slipping on my small jacket from the cockpit locker, I jammed the hacksaw inside it to free my hands. I climbed the lower mast steps, grateful that they were there, like a spare crew member. Even so, climbing up to twelve feet in such treacherous conditions summoned up all of my nerve as I couldn't focus on a horizon in the blackness. The aluminium section had split and bent under enormous pressure and it was going to take a while to cut free but not before I was violently sick with the motion of the boat.

But this was no time to be weak or sentimental about all the hard work I'd poured into our lady of the seas. In ten minutes I had cut through enough damaged metal whilst my left arm was wrapped around the lower section, hanging on for all I was worth.

Climbing back down I managed to pull the broken top end hanging down into the water up onto the side deck and disconnected the stays.

I cut the halyards.

With Grace now drifting before the wind in a monstrous sea, the motion of the boat steadied and made it a little easier to move around and conclude the task in hand.

With a heave I managed to lift the wreckage or what was left of the upper mast over the side.

With shaking hands, a pounding head and despairing at my plight I watched it sink away immediately into the foaming black depths.

I found the flashlight and checked the compass. We were drifting hopelessly eastwards which caused me great anxiety. To regain some westerly direction was not going to be easy but the uneasy thought of being pulled further into the roaring forties spurred me on. The boat was a complete mess.

I had to construct a jury rig somehow and try to get back on course but I was so utterly exhausted. But despite my tiredness I knew that every minute wasted whilst drifting, was going to make surviving this ordeal extremely difficult.

I refastened the tiller amidships then set about re-connecting the jib. Though now much lower, I could still capture some power from the never ending wind into it.

With a line port and starboard I could function it like a genoa. The mainsail was a wreck having been torn away and damaged, but I managed to somehow reef it down a little and fasten the head to the top of the lower mast at the previous location of the spreaders. Luckily the lower shrouds were still in place to steady the rig. I added a new back stay from one of our mooring ropes. This all took some time but it would have to do.

At 5.00am under a lightening sky I set the course again slightly north of west, set the jib on the starboard tack, and collapsed on the cockpit seat, a spent force.

Glancing at the current alongside Grace, I estimated that at best we were managing two to three knots, less the tidal drift of at least one knot which meant that in reality we were making probably only about two knots.

It was 8.00am 28th February and I'd slept for three hours and awoke alarmingly at the sound of the jib flapping. I checked the course and reset it. Pangs of hunger now came to me telling me that it was more than 24 hours since I had eaten anything but before I could there was still work to do. The sun was eagerly breaking behind us as I staggered below to get the binoculars from the chart table locker. The main cabin was awash and possessions and equipment was scattered everywhere. Before I could think about pumping the bilge or eating I had to take a look out for my lost partner.

Scanning the horizon on deck there was nothing to see anywhere except the deep, black/blue depths, maybe a half mile of water under our keel, and still the healthy six foot swell. The wind speed was slightly down now, but there was enough to keep Grace tracking into it and onwards towards whatever destination God had in mind for us.

With only a slight heel on it was easier to move around, a treat for my aching body.

Despondent at seeing no sign of boats or of our lost dinghy I went below to scavenge a sandwich and boiled some water on the stove to make a saucepan full of coffee figuring that I could put most of it into my two thermos flasks and keep it in the cockpit for convenience.

I suddenly realized that once I could pump the bilges clear then it would help to gain extra speed. We were obviously carrying far too much weight, and looking down at my sodden deck shoes the reality of standing in three inches of water hit me like a hammer. I was in shock. Three hours before, there was no water here at the galley floor.

Stepping down onto the lower saloon floor, the water washing all around me, I knelt down and struggled to lift the sole board trap. Constant water had made it swell and tighten up. Even so, I was shocked to see the bilge totally full of sea water. This made my blood run cold.

Pushing this discovery to the back of my mind, I climbed out to the cockpit with my supply of coffee and prepared mentally to start working the bilge pump handle.

I said a small prayer for Melanie and then one for the both of us as the pumping started.

It was 10.00am and after thirty minutes my arms were aching to extremes from the effort. I decided to continue for at least an hour more before rechecking the bilges, and for a minute I didn't even know what day it was. My mind was spinning with trying to accept the situation and start making decisions. I put the flasks of coffee safely into the winch handle pocket and climbed back down inside to check the bilge. I was dismayed to see that the level had hardly changed still washing over the floors in the saloon, maybe an inch deeper or more even after an hour's pumping.

I felt the anxiety slowly creeping over me.

Jumping back into the cockpit I lifted the access locker and stuck my head down inside to check that the exit gate valves were open to the bilge pumps correctly although in my mind I was sure that they were set correctly as the pump action would have told me fairly quickly.

But the confirmation in a way was a relief, it just meant that the pumping had to continue, all day if necessary. I downed some coffee and got set for the task in hand.

It was now midday, just before noon and with both arms aching from working the pump I took a breather but wanting again to check my progress.

Something was wrong I could feel it in my bones. Simple intuition told me that by now the floor should have been clear of water.

Surely somewhere the hull had sprung a leak during the storm.

The anxiety was ever growing within me as I reached again for the binoculars and scanned 360 degrees on the horizon. Total emptiness, nothing at all. Here I was with no power to use my engine, the radio, the sat nav, or run the electric bilge pump or use my remaining navigation lights on deck.

It was me versus the elements and now the sun was starting to beat down as Grace slowly plodded to windward without enough sail, dipping and smacking down into the southern swell.

The waves were a constant four to five feet and so I was constantly checking the bulkhead compass, trying to stay in a single direction.

My cell phone battery had long since run out of power some three days previous and in my frustration had thrown it into the galley overhead locker where it nestled with a lot of broken crockery, leaving me cursing the fact that I had not thought of buying a spare battery just for emergencies and would have cost no more than a few dollars.

I felt that I had failed Grace and of course Melanie in not taking enough precautionary measures prior to our leaving on our hopefully five to six day journey. Now it was a question of survival and only a couple of flashlights for company.

I put the binoculars away and stared grimly down into the saloon from the main hatchway. Water was moving about freely above the floors.

I reached out for the coffee again knowing that it would help me to stay awake and focus on the situation. I stared into the oncoming sea, the strong breeze cutting into my eyes.

It was time to get busy and check out the hull from stem to stern.

The last thing I wanted was to die out here. Getting run down in the dark by a large freighter was not my idea of fun, I had already survived that on one occasion but the next time I might not be so lucky.

Putting my coffee mug aside, I gingerly went down below again trying not to slip on the washed over sole boards. I was still wearing my sodden clothes and had no time to think about an alternative. I checked the hull around the galley and navigation areas but they seemed ok.

Also under the cockpit areas at the turn of the bilge all seemed ok at least until the ever present bilge water prevented going further down. I doggedly went forward searching under the saloon berths where I had stored provisions and some canned foods.

Finding it difficult to pinpoint an obvious leak, I went to the forward head compartment, finding it hard to stay on my feet as Grace rose and dropped without warning.

I fell to my knees next to the w.c, reaching to unclip the paneling which concealed the input and output valves. The latter was closed which was good though the smaller input valve was trickling a leak at the handle, though not a serious one. It also was turned off and whether I turned the handle on or off, the small leak persisted. Still it did not concern me, a minor problem.

Pushing the panel back into its place I

struggled to stand up, bilge water now washing all around me re-soaking my legs and lower body. Desperately pulling my way into the forward compartment, I cleared the berths of sail bags and baggage, personal belongings and suchlike.

It was 1.30pm.

With fear in my heart I pulled away the bunk tops knowing that surely I was not far from finding the source of my concerns.

The bows took a heavy downward smack and the bilious feeling returned to my head. The storage areas were half full of sea water crashing about at will and then I saw it.

Daylight coming through the open joints at the stem every time that Grace rose up from the oncoming waves. I turned to the starboard bunk and repeated the check. It was the same scenario, large opening joints, open to the sea and filling up our boat- the beams of light looking up at me as we crashed headlong onto our course. My mind raced as I turned and headed back to the galley and climbed the companionway steps to the cockpit to get some air and clear my thoughts. I tried to think, swigged some more coffee, and then scanned the horizon once again.

Looking at my ripped and torn sodden clothes made me wish that this was all a bad dream. I momentarily sat back holding the tiller.

Grace was a wooden boat but like any other, fill her with enough water and she would eventually go under, sink to the depths. Her iron keel would make sure of that, as had a million other sailboats before her.

CHAPTER NINE

Melanie had been dreaming. Dreaming of a safe return somewhere. She was sure that it was Port Jackson or at least that's what she would have called it 150 years ago had she lived there or came as an immigrant.

Phil was passing by near the tavern, observing her arrival with her fellow companions. She and her fellow traders had arrived to buy supplies and had come by courtesy of an English trading schooner which would be taking them back to their homeland once the formalities of their goods trading had been completed.

Now, with Phil watching her on a daily basis as she labored on the dock, she was reluctant to leave with her companions as she gradually grew fonder of her admirer in Naval uniform. The fond smiles were not enough, she wanted more time to get to know him and seek out his ambitions.

She was daydreaming but like all Daydreams, they pursue the element of truth.

The shrieking sound that made her think, only brought the pain.

The pain of letting go of that daydream. Her eyes opened, and instantly in front of her shielded by the side of the dinghy the shocking, unmistakable shape of the blue shark's tail fin slapping against her small, life saving craft, almost hitting her in the face.

She sat up in a flash, terrified of the beast playing with the dinghy like a toy. Straight away she knew that she'd made a mistake. Now she was visible and the shark could see her.

Around and around the ten foot beast circled Melanie's life saving domain. The shark raised his head to her, his eyes seeming enormous, almost too big for his head -a killing machine. She knew his type only too well.

A blue shark if hungry enough was a certain danger and if he was to catch the dinghy with his enormous tail and enough force, or land on top of the boat then his weight alone would smash the dinghy and signal Melanie's demise.

She instantly spread herself as low as possible, distributing her weight to the lowest point making the craft as stable as she could and praying that the shark was alone and would lose interest in time.

She was still wearing her life jacket and had only a small pocket knife in her shorts for protection. She gripped the thwart so hard that her knuckles turned white and she glanced upwards, the screeching sounds of the sea birds seemingly taking a strong interest in the shark's activities.

She could also judge the time of day by looking at the position of the sun, noting mentally that it was about mid afternoon and that her arms and face were stinging from the affects of the sun and the salt spray everywhere.

Again the shark turned waving the enormous crafted tail in the process.

His jaw came to the side of the boat, moving at speed, the mouth open wanting to engage upon anything in its path. Melanie instinctively stabbed the knife blade into its snout resulting in the beast reacting violently, circling the dinghy even faster. She lay back again, her heart pumping madly as she gripped the thwart.

All hell was about to let loose. Then, still clinging to the thwart she saw them.

Not one or two, but three-no, four or five Harassing the shark, colliding with him, shocking and scaring him enough to make him disappear into the depths below. Melanie gasped in disbelief at the courage of the dolphins who were now circling the dinghy.

She leaned over the side and clapped her hands, whistled to them, tears coming to her eyes in admiration. No sooner had her claps echoed into the water around the boat then they came to see her.

It was max, closely followed by Anna and Daisy who now seemed a little larger from over eating. They all popped their heads up to her and she caressed them with her hands.

She could see their tags on their dorsal fins, her 'family' had saved her life but how did they know?—They also had a couple of new friends in tow, now making a strong group of five.

The size of their group would grow massively in the months to come and would serve them in terms of security as they toured the oceans.

The air was alive with the sounds as they squawked and clicked excitedly around the dinghy, splashing and acting concerned.

They knew instinctively that Melanie was in danger. She could only assume that her group had somehow followed Grace at least up until the storm.

The activity and noise calmed down after about five minutes, then Max and the group seemed to disappear. Their hunger would drive them on regardless. The seabirds also decided that it was time to vanish into thin air as Melanie unhitched the oars, judged the direction of north by a wind check and tried to row the dinghy across the swell until her energy gave out. With the sun sinking to the west she eased up on the oars, pulled the small tarpaulin from under the cuddy and curled up to fall asleep.

The next thing that came into her mind was a picture of Phil seated in Grace's wet, windswept cockpit.

CHAPTER TEN

Wednesday 28th February.

It was 3.30pm and I was totally exhausted again, hugging the tiller and checking the compass and the horizon. I had spent the last two hours trying to stop the flow of continual incoming water at the stem, desperately combing the saloon berth lockers and checking out the tools and left over paint and sundries.

Thankfully I had found some sealing putty but despite trying to seal the ever widening gaps, the pressure was too much. The putty lasted only five minutes before giving way.

Several times I had repeated this task but with the same result. All the time the water was getting deeper inside Grace and now there was a definite four to five inches of sea water above the saloon floor. I tried to stuff some pillows or blankets into the voids but it was useless against the sprung boards of the bows. The water pressure from the waves in the seaway were far too great. One man against nature was a grueling task at best, and as I held on to the tiller trying to keep her straight, I had visions in my head of abandoning Grace and taking my chances in the life raft, but only if all was lost in trying to save her from the inevitable.

Although feeling drained and nauseous from struggling head down in the bows,
Instinctively I started pumping again, cursing the useless batteries onboard and an electric bilge pump that I couldn't use.

Keeping an eagle eye on the saloon floor through the main hatchway and with the muscles in my arms about to explode from over use, I simply couldn't stop myself from gradually drifting away. My concentration was ebbing, a sign of not eating for sure. It was now 6.00pm.

I was still completely soaking wet from my activities below and the skies were getting greyer still. The sun had disappeared but the breeze still strong, maybe fifteen to twenty knots. The five foot swells were tiring.
Grace was slapping into these waves with too much unease, a sure sign of carrying too much weight, now crashing about well above the sole

boards some six inches in depth.

I kept our heading still set at slightly north of west. I let myself fall reluctantly into a sleep telling myself that I could always eat later. The last thing I saw in the distant fading light was a sea bird I thought, soaring on into the wind as if to make statement of our lack of speed and control.

It was 9.00pm and I awoke from a troubled nightmare by the screech of a gull trying to settle onto the cabin roof.

As soon as I awakened to see him he took off into the dark void. It was amazing to at least get close to another living being albeit a large gull which of course is never a bad thing. His identity was not hard to spot, the great black backed gull is a native to these waters from New Zealand and around the Southern Hemisphere.

It also means that land is not an impossible distance away. Melanie sprung to my mind, bringing tears to my eyes and I hung my head in grief.

Grace ploughed onward, like a sodden sponge.

I grabbed the flashlight, took a quick glance at the compass and descended into the even blacker interior of the boat. I was shocked at the level of water lapping around my legs, at least four inches above my ankles , up and down, splashing everywhere with the motion of the stricken vessel. Holding on for dear life I delved into the upper cabinet at the galley, desperate for food, anything to force into my mouth. There was no question of cooking anything of course, most if not all of our fresh goods were ruined in the saloon lockers, especially the berth lockers. A lot of our provisions were in cans, wallowing around in the increasing bilge water but worst of all the issue was to save the boat, not fire up the stove.

The will to do that was pointless, for now. I found some moldy bread and a couple of apples which I soon washed down with a small bottle of water I found floating in the saloon. I was desperate not to dehydrate.

There was some moon tonight and quickly I climbed back into the cockpit to man the bilge pump. Fear of losing Grace as well as Melanie was too much to comprehend. I know that when real fear strikes, human beings are capable of some amazing things born out of self preservation. The Darkness was my fear.

Still I kept pumping, the wind now veering from south to a south westerly. My heart chilled- a sure sign that I had drifted more north than making progress on a westerly course.

I would get caught up in the roaring forties and would make no progress at all under my jury rig.

It would be the end of Grace at least and I would have to take my chances in the life raft if and when the time was inevitable. Fear was beginning to take a grip on me. I had to keep control somehow and stay organized.

It had been a long day, and now at 11.00pm Grace was pitching more than sailing, into the deep troughs ahead. With the wind tearing water from my eyes I clung to the tiller with my left arm, pumping the bilge pump handle with my right hand.

Searching ahead visually, I knew that even with a small jury rig working, the wind would strike us harder on this windward course, with a force on the port bow like a punch from a boxer.

More than anything I prayed for daylight. The last thing that I ever wanted to do was abandon Grace in the dark. At least in daylight you can see what you are doing and it's easier to evacuate.

'Dear God keep us safe at least until daybreak!'-- I can't remember my right arm feeling so disconnected from my body as the need to keep pumping occupied my mind.

I had switched off the flashlight, but felt my grip on it giving way. It fell awkwardly onto the cockpit grating but I was too tired to reach for it. Somehow it felt as if the night had come to take me, and up ahead I could hear the jib complaining of the new force to reckon with.

6.00am 29th February.

Once again I came to in a drowsy scenario, more screeching from a nearby seabird, but he wasn't a visitor, just zooming past me in the opposite direction, gliding on the gale. I glanced at the time on my watch. I'd been out for at least four hours but still felt exhausted. The sky was still grayish, sweeping black clouds swam endlessly at speed above, covering the picture like an endless dark cloak into the distance.

I was terrified at the way Grace was squatting into the wind and the mighty seas before us. My body was aching so much from lack of comfort and a lack of proper sleep.

Stumbling forward away from the tiller I crawled

on my knees at the companionway opening.

Looking down into the boat was as if looking down into a nightmare, a never ending drama that was going to end in only one way, that Grace would sink.

I grabbed the handrails left and right, gripping my way down the companionway steps. Standing on the floor at the galley the water was halfway to my knees. 'Oh my god, help me please', I plunged forward through the saloon, into the forward compartment again to see if I could force any more materials into the ever increasing gaps at the stem.

After five minutes I gave up, with the sickly feeling returning to me as I labored head down into the bilges. Water was crashing everywhere, gradually destroying the interior of the boat.

Out of nowhere an instant plan of sorts flew into my head and I waded back through to the companionway, hardly able to see the array of junk and floating debris crashing around at my feet under the water. Climbing up into the grey, treacherous day outside, I knew for sure there was only one small ray of hope before me. I was desperately hungry now, and it was plain to see that Grace was not making any headway.

She was drooping badly into the oncoming swells now. It wouldn't be long before the seas would wash over the foredeck, daring us to become a submarine. It was now 8.15am. The winds were not yet too cold but the danger was there.

Nature ruled supreme here and there was no place or time for errors, even though we were still under the spell of summer weather patterns. At sea anything can happen, and anything can go wrong and possibly will unless precautions are taken care of.

In only five days so much had gone wrong that should never have happened.

Perhaps if Melanie was with me now it wouldn't seem so bad, at least we could challenge the outcome together, but that was not to be.

Time was now paramount. I knew instinctively that beyond the tip of New Zealand's North Island, towards a latitude of 35 degrees or thereabouts one would encounter Kermadec of the Polynesian Islands, and beyond that in a northerly direction would be Tonga the main island. Both a long way off by my estimation. Further to the East lay the Cook Islands, and I'm sure that we could never make that distance.

There simply was no time and only one alternative to save Grace. That was the one thing I had to do. She was part of me now, part of myself and of course Melanie.

Around 9.00am I climbed around the decks, my wind burnt face complaining of the onslaught.

I checked the foredeck and coach roof hatches for weather tightness and gingerly crept back into the cockpit. This was it.

I counted to three in my head and swung the tiller to my left, letting the main sheet to the boom go at the same time.

With a resounding groan of aged wood she turned to north. I lashed the tiller amidships, tightened the slapping jib and let the boom out a little to starboard. Hopefully we could catch enough wind to make a course northwards and trust to God that we could make a landfall before the sea claimed our little ship. I knew that if I surrendered my hopes to the life raft, then I might never be found in this vast wilderness.

The makeshift jib was still intact though not offering much power from its reduced size and I needed every ounce of power that I could conjure up without capsizing the unpredictable hull. She was definitely unstable, carrying half a ton if not more of sea water below decks.

The more the level inside the boat rose, the more unpredictable the movement of Grace became. I was afraid that she might come apart at times, the never ending high gale wind and seas on the port side were a force to behold but at the same time, without the wind we could make very little headway and our journey would end in only one way, total abandonment.

I struggled below again to rescue a floating apple in the saloon.
The water was at my knees. I was petrified not for my plight, but for the shame of not even storing some food in the cockpit where it would have been more beneficial. Oh but for hindsight.

11.00am Thursday 29[th]February. These thoughts preoccupied my mind as I sank back at the helm, devouring the apple and working the bilge pump frantically as if that was all I was ever born for.

With a steady heel of ten degrees to starboard we pushed on, barely making five knots it seemed, but we were moving progressively. The sky was turning blacker again now and I put my life jacket back on. Everything below decks was crashing around, the water inside doing us no favours at all. Grace was moving more like a submarine on the surface, barely coping with the broadside swell.

With one eye ever on the compass I pumped for all I was worth like it was my one mission in life, a mission of survival.

After another whole hour pumping and with very painful biceps and wrists, I had an idea to make the hull more stable as I was scared that she could take a knockdown.

If she tipped too far to starboard, then the water inside could hold us down and prevent her coming up again, maybe even snapping the keel off in the process. It was a real concern.

In an instant I went below, painfully hanging on to the deck head beams and the galley bulkhead to stay upright. The water to starboard was still at my knees. I sank down to the berth lockers, removing whatever I could by way of the canned goods, transferring them to the port side, to counteract the weight of the flood on the starboard side.

Adding this extra weight to the windward side might just make the difference, stabilize the hull and make her less vulnerable to capsizing.

It took me thirty minutes to transfer all manner of things from the forward cabin as well. The sail bags, luggage, anything I could move to the port side.

Perhaps I was clutching at straws, but there was nothing else to be done.

There was a bad smell coming from the batteries location. My intuition told me that this meant that the batteries were now under water and shorting out, gradually becoming useless, redundant in any case.

I checked anyway and my suspicions were

confirmed, both batteries well immersed, with toxic fumes abundant, and the water level now up to the underside of the chart table seat. My charts and equipment were soaking wet at the shelf, personal items scattered everywhere.

Disillusioned, I wearily climbed back to the cockpit knowing that all I could do now brace myself, pump away and pray for a favourable outcome to our situation.

Grace and I were running out of time.

At around 2.00 pm I almost collapsed at the helm, I rested the pumping momentarily and took a deep breath. I figured that the fact that we were still making headway was somehow a reward for all the effort despite the constant urge from Grace to heel even more.

The seas were now long, sweeping and mountainous. There was no way to avoid this strong, howling nightmare. Only an artist would have appreciated this vast unimaginably scary and remote place. Sometimes I could see a horizon but that wasn't too often, the gigantic swells must have been twenty to thirty feet in depth, laid out like giant sweeping rollers. The noise was eerie, massive and intimidating, always relentless, unforgiving.

We were winging it, going by gut instinct. My hunger pangs were incredibly strong now, distracting my concentration but now I was also fighting to stay awake, my body drained from the efforts of the last six hours.

Looking down into the boat served only to depress and scare me, let alone hunt for any food but desperate to eat anything, I again entered down into the fray hanging on to whatever I could to prevent from falling over.

All of the galley food lockers had long since spilled their contents and the cupboards were bare to say the least. Most if not all of our food was awash in the filthy bilge water now lapping halfway up my shins at the galley floor. This only served to alarm me even more.

With my memory playing tricks on me, I suddenly remembered that there was the canned goods in the port berth lockers.

Stepping down onto the saloon floor and groping to my left on my knees, again I fumbled for some cans, all being totally submerged below. They had all lost their labels in the deluge, I would take a chance on the contents.

Heaving two or three cans up into the cockpit, I nervously clambered around to the galley area heading for the cutlery drawer.

To my astonishment the drawer had collapsed leaving only the back, front and sides. The contents were lost below in the many nooks and crannies of the bilge areas, now eighteen inches under water.

Desperately sinking to my knees, I rummaged around under the sole boards, almost submerged at times seeking a can opener of all things. It was not to be. The best that I could

Locate was a solitary dining fork and clung to it painfully with the tips of my index and right hand ring finger.

All the while Grace was pounding up, down, leaning one way then the other. At around 3.00pm and totally saturated again, I clambered up into the cockpit wielding a small hammer from my toolbox. After quickly glancing at the compass I set about trying to hammer the fork into the top of the first can I could reach.

I felt bitterly cold now, the wind was picking up again defiantly, spray flying across the decks at a constant rate.

After the third strike the fork had bent so much it was rendered useless. Staying on my knees in the cockpit I proceeded to cuss and swear at the can, beating the top of it frantically with the hopelessly lightweight hammer. My strength

And stamina was deserting me and I was succumbing to the alternative, to sleep and try to forget about food for a while if I could.

Grace was really grinding heavily now and I knew that it could be my fault from not pumping for a while.

Fighting to keep my eyes open, I realized that it was two days since I had lost Melanie overboard and the next moment, clinging to the tiller lashing and the bilge pump handle, I allowed sleep to overcome me.

CHAPTER ELEVEN

10.00 pm.

I was suddenly snatched from my sleep, into a dark noisy chasm. Grace was still moving onwards, a miracle in motion.

My head moved to starboard trying to locate the source of my awakening. There was enough moonlight to check the time on my watch

'My God,-I had slept for seven hours!'-

The noise persisted and I scrambled for the flashlight, praying that it had enough battery power. Grace's course was still true on the northerly setting. The seas were huge yet smooth and powerful, almost majestic .

A vast expanse of a desolate watery wasteland. I was reluctant through fear of gazing down into the boat's interior, knowing that it would be like a swimming pool of sorts down there in the darkness.

Leaning over the coaming, I searched with the flashlight for the source of my distraction which soon appeared, fascinated by the light beam.

A large dolphin chirping noisily, rolled around inspecting my very situation or so it seemed.

Before he disappeared, I swear I saw something to astonish me. I'm sure there was a tag on his dorsal fin but I couldn't be sure in the half light.

Quickly getting back to reality, again I attacked the food can with the hammer, this time holding the can onto the coaming to get some control.

At the third swing, Grace took a dive and the can slipped away from my grip, fell to the side deck and bounced over the toe rail into the black depths. In total despair I painfully fell onto my knees at the main hatch and gazed inside. The Flashlight beam confirmed my fears and I knew immediately that if I went down there, the bilge water even at the galley would be close to my knees.

A hundred thoughts raced through my mind the first of which was to prepare the life raft but for some slender reason, mainly the idea that preparing in the darkness was risky, I decided to reach for the pump handle and continue at least until daybreak. Then I would decide, I would have to. With midnight fast approaching, somehow I had to stay alert and pray that the pump didn't fail me.

I would pump for one hour, then gather some essential stuff for survival. Then pump again for one hour, then back to preparing bits and pieces to take with me onto the life raft.

One thing was sure. If the wind dropped which would be extremely unlikely in the Southern Ocean, then Grace would surrender to the deep, there would be very little that I could do to save her. I would have to take my chances and set myself adrift.

At around 3.00am I observed lights a long way off in the distance, maybe five to seven miles away at best and it soon became evident that it was two ships passing in opposite directions. We were still in the sea lanes.

A mixture of hope and fear gripped me for a while. I had no flare gun to hand, it would only be accessible from the life raft once it was inflated. On reflection, a poor insight on my part. Again I checked the interior with the flashlight.

The water level was halfway up the galley lower cabinets, definitely my knee level. Then I could feel that my grip on the flashlight handle was really sticky, blood seeping from my fingers, from the ever growing and breaking blisters.

Both my hands were the same and it was now that I became aware of the pain coming from them. Dismissing the fading lights in the distance, I wrapped some cloth around my right hand and resumed the desperate pumping, my fingers stinging in protest at their punishment.

With the dawn creeping at 5.00am, the blood soaked rag around my hand forced me to stop just for a moment.

I was still desperately hungry and found myself once again looking down into the boat. The sun was gradually rising from the east but it was enough to send shivers down my spine as I surveyed Grace's half filled interior. The westerly howler was picking up again but we weren't heeling any more. The hull was so heavy and fully laden that she could only manage to squat at a more or less level plane, cutting through the sea instead of sailing over it. Our speed was surely no more than three knots.

Never before had I felt so completely drained of energy but something had to be done now whilst I at least was able to move about. For a second or two I lay back in the cockpit taking in huge gulps of air, plucking up the courage to venture below again, maybe I could find a bottle of water or another apple.

In the coming daylight I could observe a large bird soaring off to port, passing over us gliding on the wind, master of his domain and like the container ship, oblivious to my plight. That was the closest I had ever been to an albatross and in a thirty second timeline and just a hundred feet above us, he was gone and out of sight. But how I envied him at that moment.

I sheeted the boom in a little wanting to catch some more of this increasing wind force.

Straight after, I somehow climbed down into the boat, slipping and sliding awkwardly. The relief to escape from the howling din outside even though briefly was a Godsend.

I was so relieved that my watch was watertight, as without thinking it had been immersed a hundred times over the past few days. I could feel that Grace had picked up perhaps a little more speed as she started to heel just a bit more to starboard.

I was falling and groping everywhere in the swamp of rubbish and debris that was once our possessions, now floating throughout the boat, enough to make me feel sick at the sight and feel of it. I could find no food nor a bottle of water, God alone knew where it had all been trapped and buried under the deluge.

Time now was at a premium and I had to face the prospect of entering a life raft with no food or water supplies to help me survive the next challenge. Cursing at my judgments in failing myself the skipper of all things, was almost too much to accept. With a grim determination I managed to salvage some perhaps useful bits and pieces and get them up into the cockpit. I could hear the jury rig complaining, all sorts of weird and strange noises transmitting through the hull going forward. I staggered to the deck , winching the jib tighter still, rather than have it shredded by the wind force. It was 6.30 am Friday 1st March.

As I started to unshackle the life raft with the wind tearing at my eyes, something unusual in the distance ahead caught my attention.

Had we passed the shipping lanes?..surely we had. I fell back into the cockpit reaching to the glove box for the binoculars.

Standing clear from the boom, I put them to my eyes and hope welled up inside me.
Land!...an island!. Way off in the distance slightly east of north. Speaking to Grace as often I did, there was only one question. 'What do you think Grace, can we make it?' My estimation was at least ten to fifteen nautical miles but there was no mistaking it, the grey, purple outline of the landscape revealed by the wind clearing the distant cloud base at the horizon.

We have to make it!

Instinctively, the only plan of action came to mind, born of necessity rather than choice. I knew that if Grace's hull failed now, that she would go down quite quickly and it would be pretty stupid not to have the life raft at least ready to use at a moment's notice.

At the expense of not pumping for a while I clambered once again to the side deck just aft of the mast and continued to unshackle the raft held in its plastic case.

I would occasionally peek through the main hatch at the water swilling around in Grace's belly. It was a horrifying sight to behold and always made me feel sick to my stomach.

With the lashings nearly released, I fastened the life raft's painter to the deck stanchion, passing it over the lifelines first and then three half hitches to the base of the stanchion.

My various bits and pieces thrown into the cockpit I quickly shoved into a small kitbag along with the binoculars and some fishing line from the glove box, anything that came to mind.

At the last minute I thought about my cell phone that I'd discarded into the galley overhead locker. It was dead now but could be useful in the future who knows.

Almost confusing myself, I worked a dozen strokes of the pump handle, cringed at the pain from my fingers, and then remembered to go down to the galley for the phone.

For safety's sake I went down backwards but after negotiating the two top steps Grace took another bow dip and my feet departed from the sodden companionway steps.

I crashed into the water below, my left leg colliding with the chart table seat.

The pain of the contact took my breath away and the next thing I knew my head was under water.

Gasping for air and from pain I staggered up somehow, keeping my body weight on my right leg, moving a couple of steps towards the galley lockers not realizing that those same locker doors had sprung open a long time ago, maybe days previous. The contents including my phone had long been claimed into the filthy bilge water.

This was just something else to cuss about, but now I could feel the outside of my left knee beginning to swell and for all accounts something felt broken. Getting back to the cockpit was an awful task, a mixture of pain and anxiety, all because I had ventured to rescue a phone that was not even there any more.

Land!

'Must check on the land'...that thought alone pulled me over the top step and then I retrieved the binoculars and scanned the horizon ahead.

'Yes!' There it was, a little clearer than before. I would not waste any time gazing ahead, I had to work. It was 9.00am.

By my estimation Grace would succumb to the ocean in about three to five hours, there would be no way of preventing the outcome.

Even closing the main hatch with the drop boards in place wouldn't hold back the rising water inside. Air could escape from the boat in many ways. The sea would win inevitably.

I kept the binoculars around my neck, it gave me a greater sense of security.

Balancing my right knee onto the starboard cockpit seat I continued pumping with my left hand, the lesser of my damaged pair, the lesser with the blood loss from the awful blisters. I had no more rag to wrap around my hands and so after another thirty minutes of pumping I was totally spent, almost crying with the pain. But I didn't panic, I had to focus with every passing minute despite the conditions.

Before clawing my way back to the side deck I took another peep into the interior of the boat. There was a lost battle taking place, and the sea was winning at a steady rate.

I groaned with despair, cussing my hugely swelling left knee.

This was it. With the wind ripping at my face and holding on for eternity, I pulled myself along the deck, ever conscious of how much closer to the sea the decks were.

Checking the painter at the stanchion, I released the final lashing and reached with both arms to ease the raft towards me.

The wind was now whistling loudly against the jib, and against the makeshift rigging. I wondered just what was holding it all together at times. Somehow Grace was holding her course, which in one way was a good thing, it meant that she was still under power albeit very little from the all ensuing maelstrom, this beast of the natural world.

It was just after 11.00 am, and with a streaking grey and black endless sky above I braced my feet apart and swiveled the life raft casing around to the lee and with an aching back, dropped it onto the foaming waters.

It rose up and down, looking suddenly small and inadequate and I prayed to Melanie as I tugged onto the painter.

With a sudden pop, an explosion of air, the casing parted and the life saving raft sprung into existence. Not knowing quite what to expect through all of my bad luck, the newfound drama of looking at the raft complete with canopy brought some tears of relief to my eyes and my heavy heart.

As quickly as I was physically able, I unhitched the painter from the stanchion and took it aft, re-securing it to the aft deck cleat. Towing it close to Grace hopefully wouldn't slow the boat down too much.

At least now I was able to evacuate, when the time would dictate at a moment's notice.

The added psychological reassurance of the life raft just a few feet behind filled me with a fresh impetus to survive as the ever terrifying thought of another night in darkness loomed ahead. It was vital to try to reach this landfall before darkness came to greet us.

Again I was all too conscious of the growing possibility of being run down by another vessel once the daylight had gone, though I'm sure Grace would sink to the depths long before then.

The compass more or less was true to course.

I fell back next to the tiller, gazing ahead through the glasses, willing Grace to pick up a little but there was nothing I could do to improve the speed of our water laden hull. I was sure that if this boat was made of fiberglass then she would have sunk two days ago at least. The buoyancy of timber was perhaps the difference between life and death.

With these thoughts running through my head I could estimate that the landfall was still maybe ten to twelve nautical miles but we were gaining, my God, we were gaining somehow!..
My hunger pangs were now beyond desperation but strangely, although I had become alarmingly thinner and bedraggled, the thought of food I suppressed as the need to pump the bilge again took over. It was 2.15pm with the wind at a steady 20-25 knots there was a chance to make a landfall or at least get close to shore before dark which would arrive around 6.30-7,00pm. I stripped my T shirt off from under my life jacket, using the material to re-cover my fingers and soon it too was soaked in blood the same as the rag before.

It was three days since Melanie had been lost and as my thoughts returned to her I questioned to myself if indeed I wanted to live on without her.

She would have wanted me to survive this journey I knew that but it didn't make things any easier. I kept looking back to the life raft.

'No not yet,--keep that pump going.' and 'Wake up,--don't fall asleep'. I was so drowsy, I hadn't eaten anything substantial for four days, in fact the day before we left New Plymouth I had lost my appetite, somewhat blaming the cause on the ensuing activities linked to our journey ahead.

CHAPTER TWELVE

With the ghosts of this journey clawing at my mind, I studied ahead again through the glasses.

Maybe ten land miles, it was clearer now, a large island.

There was a crashing sound coming from inside the saloon as wooden bunk tops were now moving about with force and I came to my senses with a sudden jolt. 'Keep pumping!'

Swapping to my left hand again, I knelt up onto the cockpit seat with my right leg. After three pumps the most terrible thing happened that threatened to push me over the edge mentally.

On that fateful third stroke the handle lunged downwards sending me reeling into the cockpit grating. The handle had become a useless free moving piece of nothing. I realized that the diaphragm within the pump had ripped from extreme over use.

There was nothing now, no pressure, no connection. The worse thing was, the pump was fastened out of sight under the cockpit floor now submerged in sea water beneath me.

I screamed in frustration, thinking 'where the hell did I leave the bucket?—yes I have a bucket I know I do!'.

It was 3.30 pm and I spun around to release the catches on the lazarette locker beneath the after deck. To my relief the bucket was there, and with a line attached.

Some relief welled through me. Like a mechanical robot I wrapped the line around my left forearm and instantly plunged the bucket into the swelling waters beneath the main hatch area. Hoisting a bucket of water was no easy task with my bloodied hands complaining bitterly but fear alone drove me on, one bucketful every dip and then to heave it over the starboard rail.

It would buy some precious time and there was no slacking now or for sure I could see her going under. 'I might have to displace a couple of hundred gallons' was going through my thinking but it might just help me to get Grace to the ever closing island.

Time was racing by now and 4.30 pm swung around so quickly. I felt I was making some difference of sorts, though inside the boat it was an increasing nightmare, a test from the devil himself. The water level inside looked as though it would come half way up my thighs if I stood at the galley. The situation was totally unreal but still I kept plunging the bucket, at time feeling as though I would collapse from exhaustion.

I prayed to the almighty again to give Grace an extra couple of knots, that we could put an end to all this misery.

My back and shoulders were aching so much now that I took a minute's rest, gasping from effort. I was just after 5.00pm, the compass was just on course and from the binoculars I took in the scene ahead through a fading light.

The island was definitely larger now, and a little more defining, perhaps six or seven miles straight ahead. I screamed at Grace not to let me down. With half a mile of deep blue water beneath her keel, more than anything I had to save her. To take to the raft now could be the end of me because of the west to east tidal drift.

At least if I made a landfall I could perhaps find some food, anything to stay alive. My arms were getting thinner and the blood soaked hands were weeping at will.

There was blood everywhere in the cockpit, stains on the woodwork and red water washing around me in a confused state.

Still I kept plunging the bucket.

Taking that one minute respite had caused me to feel drowsy, my body wanting nothing but to lay down and fall asleep.

The shortened mainsail was holding up but the jib was starting once again to protest madly, flapping and creaking as if trying to tell me it was operating on borrowed time.

I was too tired and sickly to want to venture up on deck and decided to take my chances sticking to the bucket work. By my early morning estimation, Grace should have sunk by now which meant that my hard work and perseverance was paying off. With the westerly getting stronger, screaming through the rig and hurting my ears, we ploughed on regardless.

Keeping the weight from my left leg was slowing my movements in the cockpit, but trying to ignore the pain and swelling was becoming harder as the task ahead grew more demanding.

I could see the island more clearly now, I didn't need the binoculars. I looked back to the life raft praying that I would not need it.

According to my watch it was 5.45pm. With the evening dusk approaching and sheets of seawater now coming well over the weather side due to our lower stature in the seaway, I somehow straightened my left leg to allow me to stoop down onto my right knee and resume to remove endless buckets of seawater in a swiveling painful manner.

I believe I've read several times that water is the heaviest element to carry and now I knew this only too well as the one gallon bucket kept doing its job and I wondered how much weight I was removing per hour, sadly less than Grace's hull was letting in from the bows.

I could only imagine how much more the boards at the stem had sprung as I worked my body motion with the bucket, heaving the contents overboard until I was sure that my spine would give way.

With the increasing gale from the west I came to realize that she had picked up a little more speed. Not much, but I could definitely feel it in the motion of the hull as if she was telling me not to give up.

Never had I wanted anything more than to run her aground, save her from the deep

CHAPTER THIRTEEN

The Dark sky was closing in. It was 6.10pm and fearing that this extra wind force would carry us too far east for a landfall, I had to make a course correction and set the rudder to port an extra five degrees.

This put some extra heel on the boat which scared me some but had to be endured if we were not to miss the island now opening up before us some three miles distant. I eyed the life raft still hanging on faithfully behind us.

I could faintly see rocks but we had to take whatever God would offer us. I grabbed some chord from my pocket and tied it around the flashlight then again to the grab rail on the coach roof. As the light faded, I would be able to switch the flashlight on, hoping it would be seen from ashore or a local vessel not that there would be many, if any fools out in a storm such as this.

Back to the bucket, and never had I felt so intimidated by the sea as it tried to wrestle

Grace from my grip, watching the level inside consume her relentlessly. Still we pushed on despite our decreasing freeboard.

If I had draped an arm over the rail, I could easily have immersed my hand into the sea. If a good high wave now were to crash over the port side we would surely be swamped beyond recovery.

I kept counting the bucketfuls in my head counting in tens, almost sobbing out loud with the pain from my hands.

Closer now, I could differentiate a shoreline from the bordering rocks which, although presenting a formidable barrier, would be fate's given place of landing and an ultimate shot at survival. I had to take it.

I was too exhausted and far too short of options to constantly argue my fate in my head.

As the risk and the consequences of what was going to happen built up the fear inside me, I almost passed out at the main hatch opening.

Throwing the bucket behind me I staggered upright, gazing in terror almost at the daunting task ahead to which, I would have to unfasten the tiller and try to steer Grace around a rock laden course and try to reach the sands beyond.

The sea swell now was really heavy and the boat was struggling enormously against the elements.

Strange groans and loud creaks from Grace's timbers told me that she was almost at breaking point from the waters within her, like a paper bag about to burst.

The shrieking billowing wind was much colder now, tearing at my face as I stood up, grappling with the tiller, hoping to get a response to putting the helm over.

Dark was closing in quickly and I checked the compass out of habit, and then my watch which said 7.30pm or close to.

I was running on adrenalin.

Suddenly the proximity of the shoreline was all around, small foothills in the backdrop.

I put the helm over, trying to claw more gain westerly, trying to put the rocks to our starboard side.

Grace was surely not doing more than three knots but even so, our point of contact was no more than half a mile now.

A terrifying, resounding crack came from Grace's hull and amplified out through the screeching wind as I hung grimly to the tiller. My heartbeat pounded as I saw the water now coming up and out of the main companionway.

We were going under but still had forward momentum. I had to stay at the helm at all costs, the bucket was now resolved to redundancy and rolled around at my freezing feet. The life raft was still close, hanging on for an untoward eventuality, but I didn't want it to get damaged if possible. The water lapping over the threshold of the main hatch was now starting to fill the cockpit, bringing debris and mess with it.

With the light fading I peered at the sea

beside the boat, looking even more black, deep and dangerous. I picked an opening coming up between the rocks at what seemed about 500 metres ahead.

Nothing would deter me from that spot even though Grace was now rolling dangerously to starboard and then back again to port as her groaning belly altered her behavior in the seaway. I shouted back at the wind to my left as it tried to break everything apart now, the wash bouncing back at us from the rocks, gigantic spray plumes flying into the sky ahead.

Still I kept my eyes fixed on the gap, as sea water washed freely around my shins in the cockpit.

Inside the boat was another ocean, an ocean of despair and heartbreak, of lost dreams. Like a nightmare upon us, I took a deep breath as the gap in the rocks came to us quicker than I could ever have imagined.

It was time to hang on for grim death, a time of reckoning.

With darkness upon us and guided almost by white rock spray, Grace cruised almost like a submarine into the gap.

'Come on, that's it!...come on Grace don't let me down!'...the roaring of the waves around the rocks, the sound where the ocean meets the land was all around now.

No sooner we were through the gap then I had to pick my way around the rest closing in on us. The din from the sea and the overhead gulls was everywhere but I could only guess the distance to the beach beyond as there was no sign of habitation, only the blackness for maybe five hundred metres, I couldn't be sure and I couldn't hear myself think.

Darkness was all around as I staggered forward and switched on the flashlight at the coach roof hoping that somebody might see it.

No sooner had I gripped the tiller again when Grace took an almighty crunch from below, knocking me from my feet.
The keel had made contact with rocks way below but somehow we were moving on.

Two more minutes later and an almighty collision this time from the starboard side, almost pulled us over. We drifted from this enormous frightening rock until I felt Grace run aground and immediately the boat tipped violently to starboard, exhausting her forward motion.

Screaming from the pain in my left leg, I managed to quickly release the flashlight.
With my small kitbag clipped to my belt I climbed over the pushpit and pulled the life raft to me. I said a quick silent prayer for Grace, unhitched the line and threw myself into the opening.
I grabbed the onboard paddle and gasping for air I maneuvered the raft around Grace's port side, listening to the sick sounds of wood against rock, and the sails being ripped to shreds.

It was 8.15pm and like a bobbing cork the raft would hopefully get me to safety. I couldn't see it, but I could hear the sound of the distant noisy surf not too far away, maybe a hundred metres. I glanced back shivering with shock and disbelief yet so happy to still be alive. I could just make out Grace's outline, heeled well over between the rocks, her hull being tossed around as the sea claimed her.

CHAPTER FOURTEEN

Saturday 2nd March 1996

It was a cool, grey morning with a surprisingly cold early autumn wind sweeping over the foreshore.

At around 8.30 every day ten year old Kim Fifita couldn't wait to scour the shoreline for junk or driftwood washed up from the busy sea. It was a never ending process and often heaped reward of some kind that he could exchange for a small amount of pocket money.

The driftwood he would put into small piles at the top of the tide line ready to collect much later in the day. This was fuel to keep the home fire burning at his parent's small home site one mile away.

His small dog Mickey was rushing around enjoying the space and the sweet smells of the terrain.

When Kim first spotted the raft from fifty yards distant, he thought his luck had changed to maybe a boat!..He looked around and out to sea in all directions but he could see nothing else, just the craggy, volcanic rocks punctuating the beachscape further out.

He scrambled down the shallow cliff line and ran excitedly, calling Mickey to follow. In no time he was there, and in no time at all he realized that the person in the raft was either unconscious or dead.

He tried to awaken him. There was quite a lot of blood in the raft.

With his large eyes wide open at the grim scene before him, he looked at the horizon and then ran from the beach with his heart pounding and Mickey in close pursuit.

With the sounds of trolley's being pushed around and the subdued patter of feet moving about, gradually Phil came around.

The anesthetic was waning and he was slowly becoming aware of a dense, dull pain in his left leg. He gradually opened his eyes and started to focus upon the ceiling.

'I'm alive, thank God I'm alive'.

Instinctively moving his left hand to his leg, he encountered a heavy molding, a splint from plaster, set tightly around the damaged knee.

'I'm safe', he kept repeating to himself.

His slight of movement caught the attention of the nurse at the other side of the room. She smiled reassuring him, and then walked out into the corridor.

Phil just wanted the room to stop spinning around. He closed his eyes wanting to drift away but he could still hear the grinding of wood against rock and howling of the wind, a slapping of halyards against a broken mast.

Ten minutes later a doctor accompanied by the same nurse came back into the room. Phil rolled his head to the left, thinking about the flashlight for some reason and then he opened his eyes, looking straight at the doctor.

'Mr. Lecarre, my name is doctor Simonds, it would appear that you have had quite an adventure'.

Phil clutched his left knee again and grimaced. 'Where am I, what's happened to my leg?'

'Calm down Mr. Lecarre, the upper tendon at your knee was broken, we had to operate and put a cast on to protect it. You've been here for nearly twelve hours and were it not for a small boy discovering you on the beach, I'm not sure you would still be with us, your body was so badly dehydrated and you were losing blood'.

'Thank you doctor, but where am I?'

'You really don't know Mr. Lecarre?'

'No I really don't, it was dark I seem to remember before the landfall, everything is so vague right now'.

The doctor paused to speak.

'You are in the main hospital at Nuku Alofa and I think you are very lucky'. The nurse smiled and rested her hand on Phil's shoulder.

Phil gazed at them both, trying to piece the jig saw together. 'Nuku Alofa, he spluttered- where is that please?'

'You're on Tonga Mr. Lecarre, apparently you were found on the western shoreline and were it not for the boy raising the alarm you might never have been spotted. It's a fairly remote area. He found you quite early in the morning but by the time we got you here in the ambulance, you were admitted about eleven a.m. Your leg injury was quite bad and it was easier to operate and cast it, as you were in quite a mess'.

'Now you must rest and I'm afraid you won't be walking for a week until the pain and discomfort has gone away'.

Phil somehow wished he had died, so much had gone wrong. 'Does anybody else know where I am?'

'I wouldn't think so' said the doctor, 'luckily we found your I.D. in your kitbag otherwise we wouldn't even know your name'.

'The police will be dealing with contacts for you'-

'The police?'

'Yes of course, they are just tying up the loose ends you know, and tomorrow morning they are sending an officer to take a statement from you. Nothing to worry about, but for now you should have a nightcap and get some sleep.

The nurse will get you some hot milk and some painkillers for your knee and your hands'.

He paused before walking away, 'Oh, and incidentally we will have to keep your hands bandaged for a few days, but we will change the dressings every day. Your palms and fingers were badly damaged, but don't worry for now, we can talk later. Goodnight for now, get some rest'.

Phil lifted a grateful hand from the bed cover as if any greater effort would drain him completely.

'Thank you doctor, thanks for everything'.

Twenty minutes later nurse Leann brought his milk and antibiotics.

By 10pm Phil closed his eyes and drifted away into a world of pain and confusion and the need to sleep overcame him once again.

Sunday 3rd March.

At 7.30 am the gentle clatter of trolley's again pulled me from my troubled sleep. I had always been an early morning dreamer, but this time the horror of watching Melanie being sucked into the centre of a huge whirlpool at sea disturbed me beyond words.

There was nothing I could do to save her and had to watch as the circular demon sucked her down and out of sight away from me.
Never had I felt so helpless in all my life.

'Mr. Lecarre, wake up please it's your breakfast time'.
Nurse Leanne didn't waste any time with formalities, there was work to be done.

'And how are you feeling this morning?'
I wanted to smile emphatically but the dream was so vivid and was still fresh in my head.
'I'm a little better thank you and please, call me Phil'. She was probably ten years older than me or at least that was my estimation, and a dedicated carer. She had the same golden brown skin as Melanie , a true Polynesian, gentle and caring, devoted to her job. She got me sat

up and backed up my pillows, then moved the food tray in front of me.

'Don't forget your pills after, and the policeman will come to see you at 10.00am. When you finish your breakfast press the button for me, I'm only in the next room'.

As I slowly consumed my breakfast of rice and fruit which wasn't that easy with the bandaged fingers, I tried to imagine the list of questions that the police would throw at me. I swallowed the pain killers.

In two hours they would come to talk to me and expect rational answers. Suddenly I felt the urge for some coffee and pressed the button for Leann.

After I'd drank my coffee I drifted away into a shallow sleep, my last thoughts ever dominant of Melanie and where exactly is the wreck of the Lady Grace?.

At around 10.00 am or just after I was prepared to meet my visitor. Leann had washed my face and re-adjusted my pillows. I saw the doctor suddenly appear in the corridor speaking to another man of similar age and stature, probably mid forties and wearing a light colored suit and a fedora. After they spoke for a short while, the doctor pointed into my room in the direction of my bed and my heart took an extra beat.

The police officer walked in and introduced himself to me, gently shaking my right hand from across the bed.

Leann moved behind him, placing a cheap plastic chair to make him more comfortable. He donned his hat to her, and sat close to me.

Over the next hour I painfully revisited the journey that brought me here in whatever detail I could remember clearly.

As he took notes he took my I.D. from his jacket inner pocket. The passport, my driving license and some receipts for merchandise bought for Lady Grace. I asked him exactly where I was found. I didn't know the location, but it sounded like a good fifteen kilometers away at the western coast just as the doctor had mentioned..

He sympathized with the loss of my fiancee and praised my idea of keeping the I.D.

in a lock tight waterproof bag which had paid some credit to me.

He rose to leave as I was struggling to stay awake from the affects of the medications.
'Get well soon, I will stay in touch. The doctor told me you will be here for a while'. I nodded, grateful that the questioning was at last over.

Just after the policeman had left nurse Leann came around to ask if I'd like some more coffee. 'I'm sorry to hear that you have lost your fiancee, I couldn't help but overhear'.

I thanked her for her concern and begged for the coffee, anything to get rid of the taste of pills and anesthetic from my mouth. When I finished I once again drifted away into a restful sleep with just the sounds of chickens and songbirds coming through the window at the other side of the room.
Beads of sunlight struck the wall next to my bed providing a surreal feeling of comfort and peace.

The coming days drifted by slowly but gradually the swelling of my leg receded and the pain much more subdued. It was Wednesday the 6th March and the doctor informed me that on the Friday they would remove my plaster cast splint so that gradually I could have daily physiotherapy in order to get my knee and leg working normally again.

The dressings on my hands were now changed every 48 hours and new skin was beginning to come through, the blisters and raw flesh a painful and bad memory for me.

Although I was starting to get tired of chicken and rice and fruit, my body was starting to gain some weight again much to the satisfaction of the nurse and the doctor in particular, who was receiving regular update calls from the local police department.

It was on Thursday morning around eleven o'clock when something amazing happened. I had a visitor. In fact I had two visitors. I had just settled back reading a magazine in bed when Leann appeared at the door by the corridor, with two other people.

One, a middle aged man with worn working class attire, and the other a small boy of some four feet stature, black short shiny hair, shorts and T shirt. They were both wearing sandals and were directed to my bed.

'Mr. Phil, these are the people you should meet. This young boy found you on the shore and this is his father. They have come to see how you are'.

Leann left us in peace to introduce each other and for me to express my appreciation in particular to the young boy.

We had a really good chat for fifteen minutes. The boys name was Kim and his father was George, a popular name in these parts thanks to local history.

George was a farmer and he and his wife and son worked an acre of smallholding only ten minutes apparently from the spot on the beach where I was found. With no mobile phone the man had travelled five kilometers on his moped to raise the call for an ambulance. I was so very humbled by their actions to save me and of course for coming to visit me in hospital. I was almost lost for words at times but they were so happy to see that I was ok, and George wrote down their address so that I could visit them at a more convenient time.

I gratefully shook their hands and bade them farewell for now. I had never felt so humble, and holding back a tear was not an easy thing to do. Unlike recent events yes, today was a good day for me.

They both waved goodbye at the door before disappearing into the busy corridor.
George I think had understood that I had lost my boat and that somewhere it had run into rocks although the location was obviously elsewhere from where I was found. I didn't mention the loss of Melanie, It being far too painful to discuss.
The week had rushed on by quite quickly and before I knew it Friday was upon us. I awoke in a cold sweat, tearing at the bed sheets trying to

save Melanie from the same terrifying dream, now a constant nightmare.

Leann brought my breakfast at the usual time and I sat back trying to relax my thoughts. With breakfast eaten by 8.00 am she brought me some coffee and my spirits rose up a little.

The day had begun but I would have to wait until the afternoon for the anticipated removal of my plaster splint. Leann put new dressings on my hands and the day was fairly quiet. By 5.00pm I had a new friend close to my bedside in the form of a walking crutch.

Tomorrow they would start to help me exercise my left leg and if all progressed well, I was assured it would be ok to check out of the hospital hopefully by Wednesday next. As I lay back in the bed I thought about the policeman who had yet to reappear since his visit last Sunday.

I was convinced he had written off the Lady Grace in his head.

I presumed that this was his ideal scenario of events which helped to make his paper work and working day a lot easier, and to alleviate the need to go scouring the coastline for any wreckage.

Going through my mind also was the events coming up. I would have to move into a cheap hotel for a while at least after my release from hospital. I was grateful that I still had some funds available not only to pay the hospital bill, but there would be the need of an airline ticket to get me back to Sydney.

These thoughts depressed me somewhat, accepting that what was once a dream come true had turned into a nightmare of unexpected proportions.

My parents were poor and lived in Perth, a long way from my chosen home of Sydney, New South Wales. I decided that once I was booked into a hotel then I would call them on their landline just to reassure them that I was ok. I surely didn't want to worry them Just now.

Leann sensed my depression and tried to cheer me up upon bringing a late dinner for me. Fish! at last, something I could get my teeth into.

I thanked her most graciously and before long the plate was emptied.

It is easier to sleep on a good meal, but I was dreading the return of the nightmare as I drifted off to sleep in a darkened room around 9.00pm with just a slight glow from the room next door, and the hum of the air conditioning intermingled with the sound of crickets.

These familiar sounds brought comfort to me as I allowed my worries to slip away, at least for now.

CHAPTER FIFTEEN

It was Wednesday the 13th March, a hot sunny day in Nuku Alofa.

I had found a reasonable hotel in town and thanks to a recommendation from nurse Leann, I was checked in by 10.30 am. I could not be too grateful to the hospital staff for their utmost care to me but at the same time I was restless to move on with things.

My physiotherapy had gone well and after three days my leg movement was gradually returning albeit with a big helping hand from my new friend the crutch.

Just before lunch I had barely left the telephone kiosk in the hotel lobby after calling my parents when suddenly there was a shout from the bustling street outside.--'Phil, Phil,'..To my delight I stepped outside to greet George Fifita and his son Kim.

'How did you find me here?'

Kim smiled, his white teeth flashing, 'The nurse at the hospital, she told us which hotel, we came to see you!'

This was just what I needed, to have some conversation as a break from my haunting memories. My luck was in, George had brought an old pickup truck today, having delivered fruit and vegetables to the day market.

We were all so happy to meet again, and hopped into the pickup cab, heading for a café apparently not too far away, my desperation for a real cup of coffee getting the better of me.

I actually felt guilty at the perfect location, near to the local dock. We were seated outside, pleasant sounds all around. Kim had a milkshake, and George and I plenty of coffee and doughnuts to spare all around. But I did tell George about Melanie, I had to clear my mind and I think he could tell that I was obviously in some sort of mental anguish.

There were seagulls and sunshine, music and smiling faces. This was Melanie's homeland and the pain was almost too much to bear in my conscience. I didn't even know where her parents lived. Her I.D. was lost with Lady Grace.

I paid George well for the petrol and his

hospitality, it was the least I could do as the music drifted from the overhead canopy. This scenario was almost idyllic, but for the absence of my lost true love.

Just when I felt that sure that I would live with the pain forever, I remembered that I would need to find the police station and retrieve my passport. The hotel was getting curious about my lack of I.D.

As the local news filtered from the overhead speaker George gripped my arm.

'Listen Phil, ..Listen!!..

CHAPTER SIXTEEN

I hobbled to the pickup as quickly as I was able to, George and Kim ahead of me almost clearing the path. We shuffled into the cab again.

Dare I hope?

It was a full thirty minute drive to our destination some 25 kilometres distant.
Nobody spoke much on the journey but there was hope in abundance as I looked at the concerned faces of my two hosts.

The pickup rumbled on as the sky and the horizon opened up before us. I didn't have a clue really as to our destination in detail, but I knew we were heading eastwards to the eventual ocean. We cruised past a road sign telling me that this was the Liku Road.

Without a map all I could do was make a mental note. There was no radio in the old pickup. 'Where do we head for George?'-I probed, looking at my watch now telling me that it was 12.30.

He said, 'I think we should go to the

Oholei Beach, somebody there will know I think, about the radio report'.

In about twenty minutes we arrived at the beach area, a vast yet seemingly empty place with scattered beach huts and more rocky outlooks. As Kim and his father moved to talk to various strangers, I spotted a dinghy park about a hundred yards away, my heart pounding in my chest. It drew me like a magnet, my eyes still recording the beach location, the natural beauty of this place.

The dinghy park as such didn't really live up to my expectations. George and Kim caught up to me as I wandered grimly amongst a collection of old, neglected craft and fishing boats. George looked at me.

'What do you want to do Phil?'
I wasn't actually sure at that point. We had heard on the radio that somebody was found washed up on the beach in this area and that the matter had been or was being resolved yesterday. The information was just a little vague but it gave me hope. Resolved by who?- we didn't know, and my heart was sinking again.

George suggested that perhaps we could check the shoreline for a mile both sides of our location, something that would be hard for me to do hobbling at half pace.

'Let's use the truck' said Kim, which made more sense, and we turned back around.

I purposely kept to the top of the beach line on the way back to the truck, scouring the sand dunes, ever hopeful.

Something came into view halfway back as I gazed across to the sea. Fifty yards away there was a small patch of dunes rising higher than the rest but something white and shiny caught the sun's rays.

'George look, let's check down there!'..

I was tired, and I knew that I should be resting but, driven on beyond expectation we clambered across the sands. As we drew closer I could see that there was actually three boats turned upside down against the weather, just up above the tide line.

My heart started racing again and we looked at each other.

George and Kim weren't quite sure just what I

was looking for but after walking around the first two dinghies there it was.

I sunk to my knees in amazement and joy. There on the transom of the third boat, 'Lady Grace' for all to see, slightly faded but definitely no question, it was our dinghy.

The question was, how did it get here from the location of the first storm and across the roaring forties to this place?.. It just didn't add up in my mind.

George put his hand upon my shoulder. 'We must check with the locals Phil, come on, the village is not far, only five minutes!'

'Village?'

'Yes , Fatuma not far, we ask there, they will know maybe about the radio report'.

'First', I said, 'we must check inside the dinghy'.

I clung onto the crutch as it sunk into the soft sand and looked on as George and Kim lifted the boat up onto its side. A small tarpaulin fell out, along with the rope painter. The oars were missing, and there were bloodstains on the thwarts and on the floor.

There appeared to be savage teeth marks

at the gunwales and cracks to the topsides. The clues were running through my head.

'Ok' I said, 'Let's go - I've seen enough'.

We hustled back to the truck and all I could do was pray that there was a connection between the radio report and finding the dinghy.

The chances were that there was no connection, but the thing that clawed at my mind was 'how did the dinghy get there?'.

'Maybe a spirit follow you,' said George, and then looking regretful at having said it.

He fired the old truck into life again, Kim sat between us and looked pensive, unsure. He would normally be helping his father tend the fields and this sudden and unusual distraction to his daily routines was of a different nature, too much unknown.

The pickup brought us back to the Liku Road. We turned right and soon after that we turned left at a sign pointing to Fatuma, a sizeable village surrounded by more local farming. 'Is there a police station here George?'

'I don't think so Phil, but we can ask

somebody'.

We stopped to talk to one of the locals, an older lady pushing a hand cart full of mango fruit.

She said, 'No police but only the clinic on the main street, take the second left and you will find it'.

We thanked her kindly and with the knots in my stomach ever tightening, we very soon pulled up outside the Red Cross Clinic, locals busily passing in and out of the front door.

I took a long, deep breath and looked at George. 'You'd better wait here, I'll go inside and find out what I can'.

'Good luck my friend, we wait for you'.

With the crutch at my left side, I went through the main door, only to find Kim at my side. 'I come with you, maybe they cannot speak your English!'

'Thank you Kim', I said with a tense face.

With a waiting room only partly full of locals, we approached the counter, Kim sticking to my side. Asking about information about a possible patient and without a photo of Melanie, I tried to explain who I was looking for. I still had no personal I.D. the police in the capitol still held it. My only I.D. was a business card stating that I was staying at the Sunshine Hotel in Nuku Alofa.

I needed to know simply who was the alleged person rescued on the local radio bulletin. After ten minutes of trying to explain my connection to my missing fiancee with the desk nurse and the on duty doctor, I finally got the news that I was praying for.

Young Kim was just as excited as I was upon hearing what the doctor had to say.
'Yes , she was admitted here 32 hours ago but now she was gone, apparently collected by her father, who signed her out at 8.00am this morning'. Never had I felt so much relief and anxiety all at the same time. They didn't want to disclose the address, but confirmed the surname Tupov. After some gentle pleading I was given the number that Melanie had called to alert her father.

I was beyond joy and so desperate to hear her voice. We left the clinic, and I bought lunch for my invaluable friends on the way back to the hotel. My tragedy was gradually turning to triumph thanks to them.

5.00 pm had come by after a hectic yet rejoicing day. I had allowed myself some time to come to terms with events.

After taking a shower I had made my way down to the lobby to use the phone kiosk.
Knowing that Melanie was alive and in good hands was way beyond my wildest expectations.

Yes, I had given myself some time to prepare what to say on the phone to somebody I had never met, Melanie's father or maybe her mother.

It was months since she had contacted them, probably about the time of our engagement in Auckland and so I figured they must be in some considerable shock at the recent turn of events.
They wouldn't even know if I had survived these events until they hopefully picked up the phone.

Eager yet nervous, I stepped into the booth, my stomach butterflies churning crazily.
More stranger still, my hands were shaking a little as I reached for the receiver, trying not to

drop the small piece of paper clutched into my right hand.

I tapped in the number with my index finger and swallowed hard. My mouth was rapidly becoming dry when the receiver was picked up at the other end, and I dropped the coin into the pay slot.

CHAPTER SEVENTEEN

Thursday 14th March 1996.
At 9.00 am I had coffee and toast in the small hotel dining room. There was a taxi booked for 9.30 and it was hard to contain my excitement. I had hardly slept but somehow it didn't seem to matter, I'm sure I was running on caffeine alone at this stage, looking at my watch at least every five minutes.

There were only a few other people in the room for breakfast, business visitors, some on holiday breaks perhaps. Through my tiredness I studied the characters table to table, discreetly imagining their lifestyles.

This was a wonderful, colorful place. The people were very friendly yet I felt like the odd one out, partly due to my lack of wardrobe attire. Thanks to the market next door, I could now boast two T shirts, two sets of shorts, and a pair of jeans plus the docksiders on my feet.

In fact, everything I had worn at sea was long since discarded at the hospital. But outside it was a beautiful day with the sunlight filtering through the windows and across the dining room. My mind momentarily drifted back to Grace. Thinking back to her made me feel slightly angry. I thought that I had prepared her for the trip as best I could but somehow it just wasn't enough.

Maybe I had let her down rather than the other way around. God's sweet blessing to me was that somehow Melanie and myself had survived this amazing outcome nearly 2000 kilometres from our starting point.

I downed the last of my coffee, picked up my rucksack and headed to the desk to check out. It was 9.25am and apparently the taxis here were never late to pick up a customer.

With sunshine and a fair breeze and a fifteen minute only taxi ride ahead of me we set off in a north easterly direction towards the city boundary.

There were wisps of long, white cirrus clouds sweeping the pale blue morning skies above. The temperature gauge squatting on the dashboard top next to the meter said twenty degrees, a fine day in the making but still my butterflies were rampant.

It was difficult to contain my inner excitement though in reality the thought of progressing into the future was yet to be realized. I hoped that Melanie was able bodied enough to receive me.

Did she know I was coming?-I had so many questions not just for her but for her parents also.

Their world had been turned upside down at very little notice and I could only hope and pray that they didn't direct any misgivings towards myself, still a complete stranger to them.

CHAPTER EIGHTEEN

The coffee pot in Violet's hand hovered to a standstill above my cup.

'I'm sorry, how do you like your coffee Phil?'

'Oh, black is fine Mrs. Tupou thank you'.
Samuel, Melanie's father sat next to me around the old, ornate circular cast iron table. 'My wife knows how to make good coffee Phil, a good skill to have wouldn't you say?'

Violet almost blushed, her white teeth complimenting her smile. She said, 'If you love coffee it's all in the preparation wouldn't you say honey?'

'Yes of course my dear,' said Samuel.

I nodded my head in eager agreement, 'Wonderful,' was the word that escaped from my mouth. We were sitting in the back garden, a pale green parasol protecting us from the rising sun.

My anxieties were laid to rest as gradually their acceptance of me as a person came to fruition and the increasing welcome humbled me so much.

We were only five minutes from the east coast, I could smell the sea air coming through the garden, filtering across the vegetables that Samuel had nurtured with care.

It was a place of peace and tranquility, and the beaming smile from Violet's face told me just how pleased she was to have her baby home despite the circumstances.

Melanie was sound asleep in one of the back bedrooms of her parent's bungalow. There was a female nurse in attendance and she would be staying on for a further two days as Melanie regained her strength and recuperated. I had gazed upon her sleeping but refrained from disturbing her, content in my overwhelming joy that she was ok and would be fit to fight another day.

The saline drip was feeding precious nutrients into her bloodstream, bringing her body back to its normal self one day at a time.

She had been sleeping for most of the time since her father and the nurse had brought her home from the clinic at Fatuma. It seemed that we had talked for hours, indeed it was at least 3.00 pm and with a welcome lunch long consumed, Samuel rose from his chair and patted his wife's forearm.

'I think we should give thanks for Melanie and yourself Phil', and with that he went into the building and came back with a bottle of homemade wine and some tumblers.

'I'm sure that our daughter won't mind that we drink a toast to her health, and to welcome you both into our hearts'.

Violet added, 'Phil, you must stay here, then when she awakens and sees you it will be an extra tonic for her. You don't have to go back to that hotel, you are more than welcome to stay here for now, until you and Melanie can plan for the future'.

I sipped at the wine, feeling further humbled by their kindness.

I said,'I would be more than happy to accept your generosity I don't know what to say, I mean I don't even have my I.D., the police still hold it.'

Samuel said, 'Don't worry about that for

now, tomorrow when our daughter is resting we will go to the police station and collect your papers, no problem'. He continued, 'We have a room for you here, it's not used and the nurse she sleeps in Melanie's room, that's her job'.

Gradually the nightmares of the past three weeks were giving way to new challenges but, still flashing through my mind was how to find Grace, if indeed I ever could. We were both lucky to be alive and there were still questions that needed answering.

Time would deliver those answers.

Samuel was not a farmer hence I was not surprised that he drove a car instead of a pickup truck. This was fine in my book, nothing wrong with a ten year old Corolla, nothing wrong at all.

The man was humble and he knew his place in the world. Tonga was not a gigantic place after all, maybe 100,000 inhabitants and not an overly rich or exuberant place to live.

But there was humility and friendship, a lack of social class division and this appealed to my liking of places with character, still retaining an earthly pull, yet still a sense of freedom.

I myself am not a car freak, the modern world needs more traditional values like horses, carts, and of course wooden boats. But then I always was a true romantic.

With Samuel as witness we waited at the main desk of the Police Station. Five minutes went by until the desk sergeant returned and asked for my signature in exchange for my passport and Australian driving license.

He also reminded me that in three weeks my visitor's visa would expire, and advised me to visit the Australian High Commission in town before then if I anticipated a longer stay.

It was Monday the 25th March '96.

Melanie and I had taken her old motor cycle out of the carport and come into town to extend my visa at the Australian Consulate and then rode on to visit George and his family at the smallholding. They were all so pleased to see us again.

Melanie was gaining strength and confidence day by day, and my left leg was fit enough to handle the motor bike which was a boon for us as we got our relationship back on track. The weather was so nice that we decided to ride out to Fatuma village to thank the staff there at the clinic for looking after her.

It was there that we discovered that local fishermen were instrumental at the final stages of her rescue in the bay. There were no names given and so I willingly made a donation to the Red Cross.

We rode back to the beach and I showed Melanie the damaged dinghy which somehow had saved her life. She shed a tear and we sat on the bank holding hands as she began to explain her ordeal, how she had managed to climb into the dinghy after it had become unattached and broke free from Grace's deck. Far from catching hold of the snapped line, she had over reached and fallen in. Were it not for the dinghy she would surely have drowned, as I was below deck oblivious to her struggle.

What happened next over the coming days, she told me was even more remarkable. Within 24 hours of being adrift she was harassed and attacked by a blue shark before being rescued by her beloved dolphins, Max, and his growing troupe of heroes.

I sat there listening to this story, my mouth open in sheer amazement and admiration.

Melanie said, 'They had obviously been tracking Grace and they seemed to know later that I was stuck in the dinghy.—Once the shark had given up, the dolphins kept track and guided the dinghy to eventual safety, sometimes pushing from behind and pulling by grasping the painter in their mouths. They took turns and seemed to be enjoying the effort!'-Now my jaw was dropping as I took this picture into my head and she continued, 'Once I had re-established personal contact with them they seemed guided by their mission to protect me. It was incredible, an amazing thing to witness. Most of the time I had to protect myself from the elements with the tarpaulin. Thank God it was in the dinghy or it just might have been a different story, but as for my friend's of the sea, I certainly owe them my life'....

2.00 pm. As we rode back to the vicinity of the cliffs overlook, I spotted Kim again and we stopped to talk to him.

I said, 'Kim can you remember where you found me in the life raft?'..He thought for a moment, resting his hands from the barrow of firewood.

'Yes of course Phil, I remember everything you can follow me'.

We rode on as far as we could into the sand dunes, then kept pace with him as he tracked his mind to that cold grey morning of nearly a month previous.

Still with a slight hobble, I skipped down to the foreshore and within two minutes Kim checked his bearings.

'Here, it's here Phil'.

We all stood not far from the water's edge and I gazed at the endless horizon, a combination of beach, rocks, and more beach and sometimes white and sometimes black sand. I more or less assumed that it would be impossible to locate Grace as she could have quite possibly have sunk completely.

We said a temporary goodbye to Kim and Melanie and I walked maybe half a mile south just to look for possible windswept clues.

Being down by the beach certainly raised a nightmare of visions in my head of that fateful evening even though at times it seemed a lifetime ago.

The wonderful, ironic thing from all this was that Grace had brought me back to Melanie despite the colossal odds from nature herself.

CHAPTER NINETEEN

Monday 15th April 1996.

It took another two weeks before I was able to locate the wreck of the Lady Grace.

Impossible to sight from land, she lay some twenty five feet under the surface surrounded by various large rocks. She was cocooned into her final resting place, her iron keel settled at least two feet into the soft sand base.

Structurally all together though obviously a victim of her failing planking, she looked to me surprisingly compact.

After two exploratory dives with Melanie to perhaps recover whatever we could, we decided that there was nothing worth rescuing other than some canned food and some tools that could be saved with a little work.

We found her rucksack with her I.D intact sealed into the second watertight bag.

Everything else was a sad total loss including the engine and auxiliaries. Even at low tide some

150 yards from the shore, the top of her broken mast was still eight feet below the surface with the aluminium already crumbling and corroding away.

The positive outcome was that she was not a threat nor an obstacle to anybody in the bay. Using our old dinghy as a dive platform, my final trip down to her was to cut the stainless steel rigging away with bolt cutters and bring it ashore.

The sea would claim the rest and over the coming months Kim would maybe find bits of wood from her eventually drifting into shore.

But at the moment, she was giving nothing away, in fact she looked content nestled down amongst the rocks that I had tried to steer her through.

Melanie and I both agreed that she had chosen her final resting place.

She had in fact brought me home. A new home.

With my visa now renewed life was picking up again for Melanie and I.

Surprisingly, Grace's insurance paid out with significantly more than our initial costs for her which gave us a stepping stone to buy a small plot of land. Lady Grace was written off as lost at sea.

With my carpentry experience and an eye for detail I soon found a job in town with a local woodshop.

Melanie eventually returned to her favorite occupation, assistant at the Tonga Sea Life Centre, and we were both now very happy and contented. Life was not complicated, but easy going. Somehow it didn't seem important to hurry back to Australia at least not for now and so we planned to marry and settle back into this idyllic yet challenging place.

But every now and then we would ride out to that western shore, to the place where Lady Grace lay in peace, where unknowingly she was creating a sanctuary for many undersea creatures and fish.

They would benefit from her demise. We would sit at the water's edge with the breeze in our faces and pay our respects, sometimes a tear.

Somehow we could never forget her, the same that we could never forget Max, Anna and Daisy and not just because of the storm, but because of the journey that we had survived.

All three of us.

THOMAS GATRELL

SAVING GRACE

This is the second novel by new author
Thomas Gatrell and is also available
On Amazon E book

Also available from the same author.

Keith Banner's seemingly perfect life runs aground from bad decisions affecting his marriage, his job and his sanity.
A real page turner.

SAVING GRACE

THOMAS GATRELL

196

Printed in Poland
by Amazon Fulfillment
Poland Sp. z o.o., Wrocław

61830586R00117